INVISIBLE DOGS

Charles Boyle is the author
Jack, *99 Interruptions* and
(CB editions). Long ago, poetry (Carcanet and Faber).
Fiction under the pen name Jennie Walker (Blooms-
bury). Under the pen name Jack Robinson: fiction/
non-fiction, including *Blush*, with Natalia Zagórska-
Thomas; *Days and Nights in W12*; *Good Morning, Mr
Crusoe*; and *An Overcoat: Scenes from the Afterlife of H.B.*

Invisible Dogs

Charles Boyle

CB *editions*

First published in Great Britain in 2024
by CB editions
146 Percy Road London w12 9QL
www.cbeditions.com

SC&JL

Cover: Deborah Sengl, *And Cut!*, 2012, installation (detail).
MOCAK Collection, Kraków. Photo: Galerie Deschler, Berlin.

Photo credits: pages vii, 9 and 81 (all Havana) by Wiesiek Powaga;
page 53 (Penang) by Julian Rothenstein; page 112 (stray dog tagged
with sterilisation and vaccination certificates, Havana) by Natalia
Zagórska-Thomas.

The encounter with a stray dog on page 31 is quoted from Werner
Herzog, *Of Walking in Ice*, trans. Marje Herzog and Alan Greenberg
(Jonathan Cape, 1980). The dog on a man's back on page 53 is quoted
from Joseph Roth, *The Hotel Years*, trans. Michael Hofmann (Granta,
2015). Stanley Spencer in China in 1954 on page 107 is quoted from
Patrick Wright, *Passport to Peking: A Very British Mission to Mao's
China* (OUP, 2010).

Printed and bound in the UK by CMP Books

ISBN 978-1-909585-58-4

A journey, for example,
begins with a voice

calling your name out
behind you.

— Anne Carson, 'The Fall of Rome: A Traveller's Guide'

11 April [1974]. Departure, washed from head to toe. Forgot
to wash my ears.

— Roland Barthes, *Travels in China*
  (2012; trans. Andrew Brown)

Yesterday, arriving at the airport in Bamako at 2:30 in the morning, I stopped understanding what was happening.

— Gianni Celati, *Adventures in Africa*
  (2000; trans. Adria Bernardi)

I wake up each morning and ask: Where am I? For a few minutes I do not know.

— Alan Sillitoe, *Road to Volgograd* (1964)

My room seemed too bare with nowhere to hang clothes, and five large cockroaches in the communal shower. Why was I here?

— Graham Greene, *In Search of a Character:
  Two African Journals* (1961)

I was in Hong Kong, yes, though I might as well have been in a novel.

— Jean-Philippe Toussaint, *Self-portrait Abroad*
  (2010; trans. John Lambert)

Wednesday, 1 January 1941. In the end, there is something artificial in the very fact of keeping a private diary; nowhere does the act of writing seem more false.

– Mihail Sebastian, *Journal 1935–1944*
  (2001; trans. Patrick Camiller)

Invisible Dogs *page* 1

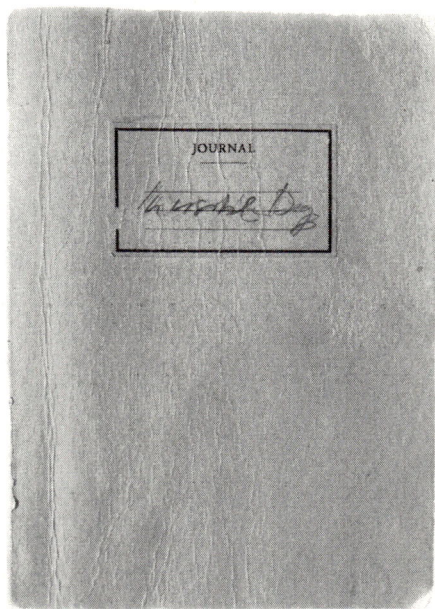

Card cover, 180 x 125 mm, 180 ruled pages.
Writing in pencil and blue biro.

People carrying things — bundles, baskets, buckets and mops, bits of wood. Books? To walk around empty-handed is a sign of status.

Sitting in a row, as if in a waiting room. All men. Shifting in their hard chairs, trying to get comfortable. So it begins, and if it ends like this too no one will be much surprised. One man had something stuck in his teeth and was picking at it with his fingers. His fingernails were blue.

The windows in the car from the airport were tinted. Not to shield us from the glare — there is no glare — but to remind me that a November afternoon in the Midlands was, is and always will be my lot. I resisted, of course. I asked the driver to open a window. He refused to hear me. Or was enjoying the music he was listening to through his earphones.

I turned on the tap in the basin in my room and after clearing its throat it vomited a spurt of tepid, brownish water . . . I'm joking. The plumbing works fine and the water is at least the right colour.

We are staying in a luxury hotel which, like every other posh hotel, puts so much effort into the *performance* of luxury it is a parody of itself. Plato wrote somewhere that the one true luxury hotel exists in heaven and all others are copies; many people believe that a luxury hotel is what heaven *is*.

The fantasy we buy into at these places is that no one has ever slept or wept or shat or made love in the bedrooms before us. All evidence of previous occupants is wiped. I have seen the trolleys in the corridors with industrial-strength cleaning agents alongside the change of sheets and towels. I have nodded and smiled at the women (always) who stand beside the trolleys waiting for the next room to sterilise, waiting to pull on their latex gloves, and they have smiled back.

Our turn will come. Meanwhile, we are on the top floor and if the weather improves we will have a bird's-eye view of the city. My room has a plant in a pot with spiky leaves and Mike's doesn't. Mike's room has a balcony and mine doesn't – his books are bigger than mine – but the door to his balcony is locked.

I dreamt of Debra, Mike's wife. Not an erotic dream, not at all. I stayed with Mike and Debra the night before we left and she saw us off. She didn't just stand in the doorway in Marlow and wave us goodbye, she drove us to the airport. I was in the back, sharing with a dog that took up most of the seat and farted. Debra parked in the short-stay, made us double-check that our passports had plenty of time on them before the expiry date and watched us go through security. She wanted to be absolutely sure that we'd left. Wanted rid of us.

Related fantasy: that of the clean slate. All previous misdemeanours erased from the record.

Blocks of flats named after 19th-century Romantic poets. On the tiny balconies: bicycles, children's toys, dead plants, a punching bag. That voice with its cynical chuckle: You really thought you could *get away*?

The first day in a new city – first hours, when I'm keen and credulous – should be as sharp as the first day at a new school: the lockers, the hooks in the cloakroom, the smells of older children, the way voices bounce off the walls in the corridors. Later, routines set in; foreground recedes to background, elaborate rules are internalised without any understanding of *why*. But here, sound is muffled and the light arrives through a filter which no one has cleaned for years. Did they put something in my tea? We are being protected from difference.

Small boy kicking a ball against a wall. Generations of this – every afternoon, until it gets so dark he can scarcely see the ball. Up and down the land: kick, bump, bounce . . . A heart pounding.

Tattoos. Essay? My agent would demand that I get one myself, otherwise it's just window-shopping. The tattoo shops – there are plenty, but they are all offering the same designs – are on side streets. The nail bars are on the main drag.

Mike told me he had a tattoo himself. Did I want to see it? No.

Schoolchildren dressed in sky-blue to make up for the lack of blue sky.

Lee, our minder and interpreter, is in his late thirties. Roughly. I find it hard to guess the ages of people back home, let alone here, where their life-battering has been different. Small frame, wiry – a jockey. Clean-shaven, very punctual, always polite. He is married and has one son but volunteers no other information about his personal life. 'Lee' is probably not his real name, just a name that's easy for foreigners to pronounce. He makes it very clear that he is working: he is not on a picnic, and we are not his friends. But I like Lee, and I want his approval.

Lee wears a yellow beret, indoors as well as out, to

make him conspicuous, so that we don't lose him, and his fingernails are not blue but bitten.

Lanyards. Name tags with little photographs stuck on them, like the photos on gravestones in cemeteries in hot countries. Or the author photos on book covers. The lanyards self-destruct on the last day of the conference; the photos on gravestones and books last a little longer but they all fade and get rained on.

Has anyone ever been strangled with their own lanyard, like Isadora Duncan with her scarf? Often, I suspect. It's under-reported.

Presentation: schoolchildren reciting poems.

They were so young, so eager, so cleanly dressed, the ironed creases still sharp. One boy forgot his lines. For a gap of several seconds that felt like much longer, and which I *wanted* to be longer, he stared straight back at us, stock still except for his rapidly blinking eyes, offering pure silence, until a girl behind him chimed up with the missing verse and the boy resumed. One of his shirt buttons was also missing.

We – Mike and I, Lee, the head teacher of the school, half a dozen others in suits – were sitting in the front row, reserved seats, but everyone knew that Mike and I were really the kids in short trousers.

The welcome speeches came at the end – I assume the

schoolkids were too eager and couldn't wait to begin. I wasn't sure that I could wait, either: I was dying to go for a pee. Each speech was longer than the previous one, and the way each speaker's intonation started to suggest closure only to spark up again was a form of torture. I tried to catch Lee's eye but it was like trying to catch a waiter's eye in a busy restaurant.

Exhaustion: essay? And bladders.

The kind of suit worn by a premier-league footballer when he walks into court to face a rape charge. And his minders, and his lawyers. School uniform. When they get home they'll change into something more casual.

Canteen food, quantity over quality, food as fuel. But *good* canteen food, with the taste of mum's cooking. Whoever is preparing the food still gives a damn. Mike keeps asking for more salt but it doesn't need it.

A woman at the next table peeling an apple, with great concentration. Domestic erotics.

The national soup, ubiquitous. Moustaches are flecked with this. Moustaches are also ubiquitous. Some women have them and they are not unattractive. The soup is offered under many names but it's the same soup at different consistencies, depending on the proportion of beans, and different temperatures, from chilled to scalding.

Also the national soap. It does the job.

The national shrug. The answer to almost any question: What time does the train leave? Do you believe in God? What *do* you believe in? What's actually in this soup?

We are asking the wrong questions, or addressing them to the wrong people, or only some questions — not many — have answers. Or there is a list of questions that they are allowed to answer along with the officially approved replies but no one can find it or remember when it was last updated so the response to all questions is defensive.

The shrug is both expressive and elegant, especially when it's done with an apologetic turning-out of the hands. The hands are invariably very clean. A shrug *is* a kind of cursory washing-of-hands.

And it's catching — I am starting to use the shrug myself. It's a simple upper-body thing, the legs don't budge. If you do it while walking it's a dance move. I practise in the bathroom, each wall of which is a mirror, so I can see myself from behind.

No electric kettles. No deodorants. On the other hand, there are items here which back home have lapsed into oblivion: carpet beaters, fly whisks.

Certain types of character have also lapsed. When particular professions vanish, overtaken by technology

— troubadours, cavalry officers, chimney sweeps, bus conductors — the ways of encountering the world that come with those livelihoods, the mental ways along with the physical, also vanish. As with genres in music and film and literature. Novels?

Mike, two of whose children work in IT — how many does he have? — tells me I am being sentimental. It's a revolving stage: exit old characters, enter new ones.

I haven't read Mike's latest book, and I doubt that he has read mine. I have read some of Mike's reviews, and I have *browsed* in Waterstones, but life is short.

Dogs. There aren't any: no one keeps them as pets and strays have been rounded up and shot. A problem of public hygiene, Lee says, which the government has taken care of: now, no dogs, no disease. What about rats? I asked. Don't stray dogs have a hygiene *benefit*, keeping down the rats? Also no rats, Lee said.

But I keep seeing dogs out of the corner of my eye, at the edge of vision — today, trotting on the other side of the street, then scarpering around a corner. Yesterday, a dog with only three legs was skulking in the loading bay of a supermarket, where the food that's gone off is dumped in skips. Their movement is whip-sharp. Even if it's just the movement that catches my eye and by the time I've adjusted focus it's too late, that dog was *there*. Officially there is also no hunger.

I asked about snakes and Lee clammed up. He was on such a positive roll and now he will have to check with his superiors before he gives us the line on snakes.

I know better than to photograph the dogs. The new national library, fine, but if I try to take a photo of a beggar — the abject ones hunker down, the aristocrats pose — or rubbish on a pavement or even a patch of peeling paint, Lee becomes agitated. Mike says he could lose his job. I don't think it's fear; I think Lee feels a deep and personal sense of shame. Not because dogs and rubbish exist but because officially they don't.

'Resistance to an off-the-peg aesthetic.' That sounds so prim. Resistance to this journal acquiring the tropes of fiction.

At the national library an archivist showed us centuries-old illustrations that mapped the body politic onto human anatomy. We put on gloves, like servers at the fish counter in Waitrose, and were allowed to handle them. The king was the heart, obviously. The lungs: landowners, fishermen, rhetoricians, aeronauts and balloonists. The liver: lawyers, doctors, graphic designers. The kidneys: policemen and public executioners. The bladder: actors, bailiffs, estate agents, traffic wardens. The anus: chimney sweeps, night-soil collectors and assorted criminals. At various points along the intestines, accountants, blacksmiths, postmen, bus drivers and middle managers.

Writers? Probably included under 'rhetoricians', said the archivist, but she looked doubtful, as if we'd snuck into too high a caste.

Archivists? The intestines, which are a catch-all.

Beauty of hand-drawn illustrations. Even when of something vile.

Mike pointed out that the anatomy depicted in all the drawings was male. He had to be looking closely to say this because generally the drawings were gender-neutral, one-size-fits-all. The archivist, enthused by our interest, told us about heretical drawings depicting the body politic as female, and the high prices these now fetch at auction.

Mike had a coughing fit. *Cough-cough-cough* and then wheeze, and go again. He was choking something up and I imagined a frog with blinking eyes and not just one of them, there was a whole queue.

Internet issues. And phone. Not the connection, but what we are permitted to receive and what not. This varies, depending on the mood of whoever is on duty in the control room, whether they are hungover and crabby or have fallen in love and are feeling generous. Or what they've had for lunch. Some days Mike can get the cricket scores, other days not – this determines his own mood for the rest of the day.

Mike has a cricket bat standing by his bed. Does he take it everywhere with him? Of course he does, he never knows when he might need it. Lots of people keep baseball bats in their bedrooms but Mike is English.

Should I be watering the plant in my room? It looks parched. Today I asked the woman who came in to change the sheets: I went to the bathroom and filled a glass with water and poured it into the plant pot and looked at the woman in what I hoped was an interrogative way. She shrugged. It occurs to me now, later, that she may have thought I was suggesting – in that roundabout way that men have, trying it on while pretending not to in case it goes wrong, she is used to that – sex. The plant was there on the day we arrived and I felt awkward about it being there, and I think the plant did too, but Lee explained that our arrival coincided with a national holiday on which people give flowers and plants to celebrate, so I couldn't tell them to take it away.

Pale, watery sunlight. No wind. Trees utterly still, standing around with nothing to do. Day-labourers waiting on the pavement for the man in a van who needs a couple of brickies but never turns up.

Men wearing trousers with wide flares – nautical. Like sails.

Mild indigestion. Nausea. Sea-sickness.

Lee gave us some local currency, coins and banknotes. Not that we'll have many occasions to use it; we are embedded, like journalists in an occupying army. An unfamiliar dish: Mike sniffed one of the banknotes and then he put it in his mouth and chewed it. He was fed up with being treated like a schoolboy and given pocket money for good behaviour. Or his intended message was that he wasn't afraid it would poison him; or that he was down with the kids and capitalism sucks. Whichever, he had totally got this wrong. Lee was embarrassed, I was embarrassed, the waiter was more than embarrassed. He accidentally-on-purpose spilt a whole cup of coffee onto Mike's crotch. There followed a discussion about the toxic chemicals employed in dry-cleaning.

Dear hotel manager — Thank you for your note assuring us that every effort is being made to make us feel 'at home'. We too are trying our best. It's not easy, in a hotel dedicated to a corporate international style with a few token 'ethnic' artefacts in locked cases in the lobby. And having to pretend not to see any dogs. I don't want to appear ungrateful. The coffee is excellent.

It's like boarding school, Mike says, and the comparison excites him. Each day of the week chopped up into time-tabled portions of alternating tedium and frenzy, point-less except to reduce any leftover time to tiny pockets too short to ferment (foment?) anything interesting. As if days are wild things — which they are — in need of vigorous masculine control. Supervision. Discipline. Plenty sticks, few carrots. Bells, gongs, cupboards, keys. Petty rules like invisible trip wires. Sex? What's that? Or, You'll be lucky. Power held languidly but abso-lutely, riding crops gripped tight behind backs. White knuckles. Child abuse with charitable status. Neither side benefits from this but neither side knows how to get out of it. Great bowls of burnt porridge.

I went for a nap after lunch and when I woke up it was dark and I'd missed the main event. Mike said I hadn't missed *much*. But that's not the point.

Which of us will die first? I often ask myself this both about people I know and love and about the stranger standing next to me in a bus queue. All things being equal, and given a level playing field, the older person will die first, but no playing field is level.

Lee asked me if Mike snores and I told him that is a rhetorical question, and then wondered why he was asking *me*. But not for long because I had got into my head that old trope about dogs' owners resembling their dogs and I was remembering the dog that slobbered and farted on the back seat of the car on the way to the airport.

Tourists: lightweight clothes, sensible shoes, a spare pair of glasses just in case, ticket-anxiety and adapter plugs, an app on the phone for translating menus. They *amble* on busy pavements. When they cross the street they wait for the little green man because they are never quite sure on which side of the road the traffic drives. They have forked out an arm and leg for insurance in case they lose an arm or a leg so if they do lose one of them they are going to be quids in and they have two of each, one should be enough?

Familiarity of the light in mid-afternoon . . . *Slow Mercy*, good title for a book, not by me but I might read it, or begin reading it.

We are not here for long, things don't have to be perfect.

Among the flyers for tourists at the hotel reception desk: the ice-cream factory, the museum of colonialism, the museum of anti-colonialism, re-enactments of famous murders in an intimate setting.

Constantly switching between languages, Lee is a croupier in a casino, gathering in and paying out, or shuffling a pack of cards very fast.

He is always busy, always anxious. Playing catch-up. A larger man would be slower and less anxious, but a large man would not have Lee's job, he would be seated behind a desk. In his downtime Lee takes out a notebook and makes sketches of Mike and me. The drawings are realistic but with more than a touch of caricature, like the drawings a pavement artist might make of tourists. *Affectionate* caricature – the artist does have to make a living. When we leave I hope Lee will let us choose a couple to take home. And in return we will give him beads, cornflakes and Christianity.

There is a damp patch on the carpet in my room. A mystery: not near the window, and nothing dripping from above. Odourless, so not urine. Believe me, I have been on my knees, sniffing.

More lanyards today. Along with bottles of warm water, free pens, and pads of ruled paper to doodle on. Scrape of chairs around the table on the pretend-wooden floor. Lukewarm coffee. Chitchat while waiting for late-comers: the weather, the bus strike, a bug going round. Apologies for absence. The agenda for this morning. It's like being a child in a Protestant church with a vicar with a handkerchief tucked up the sleeve of his vestment. Bad lighting, bad acoustics: this too is an aesthetic.

What will survive of us? Not for us to say. Meanwhile, we go through the motions of a ritual whose meaning can only be guessed at, as if we are already in a museum.

'Lives of quiet desperation' – but not Mike, who likes to turn up the volume.

Even the clock dozes, then jerks forward, catching up with itself. A scratching behind the skirting boards – mice? Their tiny, jewel-like turds. Framed in the window, fluffy clouds, a bird flying past. We were lucky to have a window, Mike pointed out; most of these rooms are in basements.

I was tonguing a wobbly tooth: like picking at a scar, an addictive pleasure because sometimes sharp – testing the border between pleasure and pain – and because it tastes of *me*.

I was a comfortable child. Sometimes when I woke up the water in the glass by my bed was ice but I don't remember ever being cold. I remember certain clothes that I wore half a century ago, not just how they looked but the touch of them. Perhaps too comfortable, but this is not a complaint.

One day slides into the next and though he tries to hide it, I can tell Lee is pathetically grateful when things don't actually go wrong: when the lift isn't out of order, when our driver turns up more or less on time. When he presses a switch and a light comes on.

Sometimes I feel the blanket impoverishment of the senses, and the dulling-down of all aspiration to *getting through the day*, must be deliberate, but that would make me a conspiracy theorist. Other times, for no good reason, I feel almost *blessed* to be here. An accident? A mistake? Like I am being stroked.

My mood zips up and down without warning. Mike is (a) an awkward but genial fellow-traveller whose jokes are half-funny and (b), damn him, he is dragging me down. And damn Lee too – I am fond of him but I am not responsible for him. And damn *me*. I am wasting my life. The melodrama of that sentence – pompous, self-centred – makes it even worse.

Rome is an earthy yellow. Dry but not parched, and not the yellow of buildings in more northern cities, where the light is different. Paris is blue. Dublin, unexpectedly, is pale pink. Tashkent, where I have never been, is a subdued violet. London is pigeon-grey. This city is also grey but a more uniform, concrete grey. Heated discussion on this at the Writers' Union; much disagreement. Writers too can be plotted on a Pantone chart: purple writers, orange writers, beige writers . . .

From the car on the way back from the Writers' Union I saw a woman on the pavement with pale skin and red hair and I knew I had seen her before, perhaps in the audience at one of the presentations. I am convinced she is Scottish. She has freckles, I think, but I only saw her in passing. She reminds me of those Englishmen in the 19th century, women too – and this happened before then, and still does – who went to live in an Arabian desert or somewhere far, far north and that was the last anyone back home heard of them unless they wrote *books*, which very few did. They had chosen to disappear and most did, without trace.

I'd like to talk with this woman, if only to hear her voice and confirm that she is Scottish and has freckles.

As a concession to our status as honoured foreign guests, the hotel management has informed us that if there's a fire drill they will let us know in advance and we can stay in our rooms and not have to stand around in our pyjamas at the assembly point. But what if they forget to tell us? If the fire alarm sounds, I tell Mike, we should always assume it's for real. Mike says I'm being paranoid and that every alarm will be a false alarm. They are not going to let us die here. Bad publicity.

I'm disappointed. I wouldn't volunteer for more than my fair share but as long as it's not raining I enjoy these companionable rehearsals for disaster — waiting in the car park with strangers or work colleagues while someone checks that everyone has left the building, small talk and plans for the weekend. Time out.

Lee showed us prints of the official photographs taken at the Writers' Union. Mike has gravitas, a writer to invest your life savings in; I have an inane grin, wanting to be liked. In life we reverse roles, but I still lose: Mike looks jovial, exuding a perfume called Bonhomie, while I look worried, as if I've forgotten something, as if I'm always forgetting something. I have this habit — people have noticed — of glancing into corners, or along shelves that need dusting, as I walk by, as if whatever I've forgotten might be there.

The photo in which my eyes are closed is best, but it's not me who gets to choose. I sign off. Someone who wants to be liked doesn't make a fuss.

I slept well. I missed breakfast but I feel well rested. What did I do to deserve this? Probably nothing, but in case it was something I'd like to know, so I can do that something again.

Good sleep makes for good balance, appetite, judgement and accuracy. If I was going to kill someone I'd have a nap first. And then take a shower. It will be an afternoon. No rain, a light breeze, and clean clothes: these pants, those socks. There are standards to maintain. Contract killers – the reputable ones, the ones with testimonials on their websites and who can claim for expenses on their tax returns – don't come cheap.

I could take that back but there is no *back* to take it to.

It was important to wear clean underwear in case you got run over by a bus.

A large part of the high-protein diet we are being fed is statistics: cubic metres of concrete, numbers of construction workers, grain harvests, temperatures, birth rates, literacy rates, tonnage. The world reveals more of itself when you dig beneath the numbers but you have to start *somewhere*. When we talk with other writers the first questions are always about print runs, sales figures, money.

Selected statistics, we know that. How many people kill themselves? How many are in prison? How many keep dogs illegally in back rooms? How many people's lives are deformed by (a) poverty, (b) wealth, and (c) regrets?

I asked Lee about poverty and he came back with the official figures but they know they can blind us with whatever numbers they want and we won't answer back because it is *a truth universally acknowledged* that writers don't do numbers because writers think numbers are for geeks and geeks are boring and the one thing expected of writers is that they not be boring. I sincerely regret not paying more attention in class to Mr Jackson.

For the record, Mike's books sell more than twenty times as many copies as my own. And he puts out a new one every two years. And he drives a BMW. And the very successful film made from one of his novels has raised his status not just among people who have never read a page he has written but on the book pages too.

I am jealous of Mike. For all the wrong reasons.

The streets are decorated with squashed pigeons. I think they trust in numbers. Individually, they are pretty stupid. Many are so fat they can barely get off the ground. Without dogs to chase them, they think they don't need to.

Lee is our dictionary: alphabetical, unflappable.

Having to rely on Lee's translation means that we are locked out of what is happening around us. Or a dimension of that. Or rather, there's a delay on the line: we don't get the message live, and other messages are stacking up. This may not matter. Not being able to read the headlines, the ads, the posters, or comprehend the public announcements, feels like a release from the burden of meaning.

Because we have different vocabularies we speak the world with different colours, sounds, flavours and shades of feeling. That the differences may be slight means that often I think I understand what is being said when actually I don't. I spend most of my life *almost* understanding. In my hurry to get there I tend to jump over gaps that only later become evident. It's like dating, I imagine.

To truly understand another person *all the time* would be unbearable. But moments of true understanding can be occasions for delight, like getting the point of a joke.

If the Scottish woman has gone native, as they used to say, then she eats, drinks, dresses and smokes as the locals do. But it will take generations to make the full shift, which is often most evident in a culture's sense of design (film posters, menus) and in what they find funny.

Mike, who smokes cigars, has discovered that the alarm or sprinkler in his room is just for show and he is puffing away merrily.

Mike has got the key to open the door from his

room to the balcony. He has leant on someone. Dollars were involved, and a promise not to throw himself off. Though he didn't sign anything and he might change his mind, he says. Last night, before turning in we sat on the balcony with glasses of whisky and it felt as if we were smoking behind the bike sheds.

The city is endless. Arteries, pulsing lights — a live scan of a human body. Trite metaphor. Directly below us, half a dozen men were clustered around a brazier on the pavement, warming their hands. Maybe cooking something (a dog?).

They ran wild in packs. They spread disease. They fouled the pavements. They kept us awake and then infected our dreams. They bred faster than rabbits. They *laughed* at the police. Whole districts became no-go areas. Finally the government took action: they were rounded up and slaughtered and buried in pits and now there are no dogs (officially). Soon — a generation? — there will be no artists or writers. The government will be forced to take the necessary measures.

Oh, it won't be as bad as that, Mike assures me. Tourists like them. They add local colour, they make the place look *authentic*. A small number of writers will still be permitted, tagged with the numbers of their sterilisation and vaccination certificates. If they have a good agent they will do well.

When people reach a turning point they don't realise that they have passed it until they find themselves heading in an unfamiliar direction. Delayed recognition, as after a car crash or a stabbing in the street: among witnesses that moment of shock – a hole you could vanish into – before realisation that yes, the curtain has been rent.

Watching strangers here walking the pavements, I imagine the people walking in the street back home, where I am not, and then myself back home imagining the people continuing to walk the streets here, without me. A childlike feeling of suspension – the sheer strangeness of me being me, here, now. So strange that it seems I have to imagine myself somewhere else – or some *time* else – to get a fix on this.

A vice-president has arrived, or maybe just a trade envoy with a chequebook, and the streets in the centre of town were closed so we had to take the metro. Lee was nervous. Whenever our schedule is threatened he fiddles with his collar and pats his shirt or lapels, as if trying to brush something off. Dandruff? *Dog hairs?* I reassured him – we know we are just an add-on, we are used to waiting in line – but he was still nervous. If things go wrong with us he is not going to be promoted to minding the trade envoys and the vice-presidents.

Impressive, triumphal entrance, less so inside. We saw a youth vaulting the turnstiles with exemplary athletic skill and then being arrested by security staff. The train was busy. A shuffling of bodies left Mike, Lee and myself sitting down and three previously seated passengers standing up. Facing us were students, an office worker, a woman who might have come up from the countryside. They stared at Mike and me like small children, without a trace of self-consciousness. We were fruit in the market — what they really wanted to do was to prod us, to press their fingers against our skin, to find out if we were ripe or still hard. You can't decide whether to buy or not until you know that.

The country woman had a young child with her, a girl in a pink silk dress, a party dress. She stared, but when I looked back at her she turned and buried her face in her mother's black skirt. And then peeked back, when she thought I'd stopped looking.

Do baboons in the zoo feel more self-conscious of their baboon-ness when they are being stared at than they do after the visitors have gone home, after closing time? (There is no zoo here. We are the zoo.) Is this what makes them thrust out their pink bottoms and make that screeching noise? At night they may be very quiet, and shy.

Cranes during the day perform a slow-motion ballet, awkwardly — thrust up into public view, they too are quite shy, really. They didn't set out to be phallic, just to perform a basic mechanical task. At night they wear dinky red lights. Canis Major: if I join up the lights on the cranes I can see from my room I find that I have drawn a dog.

Tooth fell out. The root was long dead. Flecks of blood, then nothing.

Had my shoes re-heeled by a cobbler. I stood in my socks on a grubby mat while the gluing and hammering was done. I had left my pocket money back at the hotel so Lee paid and now I owe him a trifling (but not to him) sum of money and this was days ago and I have only just remembered. Welcomed and applauded and driven around in flash cars, I am not a good person. Soon – I don't know when, but soon – they will realise this and take me down. Adulation corrupts (ask any deity).

I keep seeing faces that feel familiar. 'Harry?' – I said this to a man in the hotel lift, going down, when we made eye contact. He looked terrified, as if I was accusing him of wife-beating. Maybe he does beat his wife. The woman he was with stared at me fiercely: KEEP OUT. Harry was a quiet, patient man I knew decades ago, an entomologist who collected first editions, and this was Harry too, though of course it wasn't. There was something of James Mason in there too. No wonder we were both confused.

Mike and I gave a reading from our recent books. Mike wanted us to read from each other's books, not our own, to see if anyone would notice, but I said no. For Mike, the highest genre is not epic poetry or literary fiction but the practical joke. The professor who was going to introduce us reminded me of Mike's wife: she warned us that if we overran our allotted time she would cut us off in mid-sentence.

We watched the audience coming into the hall. As usual, the rows in the middle and towards the rear filled up first. No one wanted to sit in the front row. Did they think we would splutter and spit? Were they worried there might be some kind of audience participation? Did they think they were at a funeral, and the front seats were reserved for close family?

In the fourth row back there was a man aged at least a hundred. The seats on either side of him were empty. I don't think he was smelly – he was well turned-out, dapper. Maybe he had nothing interesting to say, or everyone had heard all his stories too many times. Maybe people just found his being so old a little scary.

While Mike was reading Lee followed the text in a copy of the translated edition of Mike's book. His head was down but I could I see the tiny movement of his eyes from one side of the page to the other and then down and back, a controlled trembling. Hummingbirds.

Just before I began my own reading there was a

moment when the page went blank and, like the dogs, everything I had written did not exist. I blinked and swallowed hard. I looked out to the audience, hoping to see the Scottish woman.

Questions from the audience: Which writers have influenced you? How long is a novel? How do you choose your characters' names? What is your opinion of Victor Hugo? What are your books about? Can art save us? (No. *Then why are you here?*) Are you rich? Are you married? What is a ghost writer?

Mike charmed them. I had no idea he could waffle so plausibly about Victor Hugo.

I am the spare. In case Mike overheats, or falls down a sinkhole.

Greetings and numbers comprise most of the language we are picking up. Whole lives may be lived with just those. *May you live for as long as a tortoise.* Dollar conversion rates. Lee could be more helpful but is reluctant to engage in anything outside his job description, anything that might involve intimacy. He scratches his collar.

Could we be learning more of the language from the wide-screen TVs in our rooms? In practice we learn no more than what we knew already: floods, fires, famine, football.

Even Mike, who knows his baseball from his football, his chess from his beach volleyball, was baffled. The match we were taken to see at the national stadium was more football than cricket but sometimes the players used their hands and this was OK and sometimes there were two balls on the pitch at the same time. Lee's explanations were an extension of the game itself, prolonging our incomprehension. We had to deduce the rules from the stops and starts, what was cheered and what booed, but each time we thought we'd got a hold on what was good play the referee blew his whistle. I have no idea which team won. Maybe the rules are there to be *bent*, and players are applauded according to how elegantly or outrageously they do this. Maybe taking our cue for understanding from games we already know is not what we need to be doing. Maybe the point of the game is not to win but something else.

Lunch today in a college canteen. Soup. But also fish: caught just yesterday in one of the up-country lakes, we were told. Lots of tiny bones. At the next table a group of well-heeled bandits were staring at spreadsheets. At the table beyond the bandits, facing me, was the Scottish woman. She does have freckles. Briefly, we made eye contact. But then Mike insisted on showing me a sketch that Lee had made of him and when I looked up again the Scottish woman had gone.

The visit to the recycling centre was cancelled at the last moment so we went shopping for presents to take home. Nothing large, we told Lee, and nothing heavy. We came back to the hotel with a selection of vintage egg-timers made by master glassblowers in a region known for the fineness of its river sand. In fact the sand is quite gritty and sometimes gets stuck in the neck between the two glass bulbs and you have shake the timers hard to get it through. They are ornamental rather than functional. And fragile, so we will need to wrap them in yesterday's newspapers.

But this *is* how time works: running fast, running slow, and sometimes it gets stuck and you have to shake things around to get it flowing again.

Mike also bought a worker's hat and a pair of tight-fitting black gloves, the kind you wear when you don't want to leave any fingerprints.

Dogs not seen but heard – a snuffle, a whine, a whimper, a patter of paws on a hard floor. Rarely anything as emphatic as a bark.

Lee checks his watch so often that for a while I thought his boss must be using it to send him traffic updates. I was wrong but I was also right – Lee has to get us from a factory to a school to a concert hall on schedule, so behind his nominal boss back in the office his real boss is time. Fingernail-biting and collar-scratching for Lee, and we do feel rushed. Rushed to where? Beyond just the next stop on the itinerary, we don't know, and nor I think does Lee. We'll only know when we get there, but the more we rush, the further away that place gets.

We are stuck in a loop. It will take an earthquake to get us out of it.

Feeling of being watched, graded, marked out of ten. Continual assessment. And then Mike says, he's not stupid: What if no one is watching? What if no one is paying any attention at all? Why would they be watching us rather than the football?

In November 1974 Werner Herzog began walking from Munich to Paris, where the film curator Lotte Eisner was seriously ill – he believed that his journey would keep her alive. A pilgrimage. Beside a muddy field in northeastern France, he encountered a stray dog: 'I said woof to him, then he immediately came and followed me. When I looked back at him several times, he didn't want to be seen, and he just trotted behind me in the roadside ditch. It went on like this for many miles . . .' Eventually the dog wandered off. Or rather, when Herzog looked for it, he couldn't see it. Later in the day Herzog entered the village of Brienne, where 'people started to hide at once, with only a small grocery store staying open by mistake'. Above the town stood a castle ringed by a high fence: 'That's the insane asylum.'

Mike called Lee and told him we were both ill, food-poisoning probably, we shouldn't have ordered the shellfish, nothing serious, give us a day in bed and we'll be fine by tomorrow. We skipped out of the hotel and headed on foot into town. This wasn't easy: the hotel is a film set separated from any streets that actually smell and sound and feel real by a six-lane highway which discourages any means of getting around except taxis and places the hotel's occupants in quarantine. Mike was so eager he nearly got run down by a bus – I pulled him back just in time, in effect I saved his life and one day he may thank me for it. It was nothing, Mike.

We found ourselves in a street market selling clothes and household stuff, pans and brushes and power tools. Tables stacked with oversized underwear – odd, because Lee's slight, wiry build is typical here, there is no obesity – and those trousers with wide flares. A bald man selling hair oil. A blind man selling sunglasses. A man on crutches selling running shoes. A table stacked with jars of noxious-looking herbal infusions and an array of lucky rabbit's feet that when I looked closely were dog's feet, and it was here the trouble started. Mike picked up a dog's foot and attempted to buy it. The woman behind the table shook her head vigorously. Then Mike took out a wad of dollars and we were surrounded by jostling children and men who were shouting angrily. Someone blew a whistle. (Mike, when we talked through it later, said he heard no whistle. I think he is a little deaf.) Two not-shouting men pulled us away – very firmly: they had been trained to do this – and stopped a taxi and took us back to the hotel. That the crowd went silent and stood back to let us pass suggests that they recognised the men as undercover police.

I felt chastened. Mike was happy as Larry: he had managed to pocket one of the dog's feet from the market. A trophy: he will take it home and frame it and hang it on the wall. His dinner guests will stare at it blearily and Mike will pour more wine and tell his traveller's tale.

A journalist – female, late twenties – came to interview me. She speaks fluent English, so Lee got time off, and we found a quiet corner of the hotel lobby. She had a list of prepared questions, none of which had anything to do with my writing. What am I frightened of? I must have looked puzzled, because she gave it another go: What gives me nightmares? Doughnuts. I think she wrote down 'spiders'. What makes me laugh? I said I found it funny that after choosing a quiet place to sit there turned out to be some serious plumbing or tiling going on behind the door we were sitting next to. Pardon? she said. I waited until the off-stage drilling had stopped and said it again. It was her turn to look puzzled. The famous English sense of humour.

She changed tack: she asked about the UK. Do men wear hats, and how many different kinds of animals are there? Questions no more silly than those I ask about her own country. She also asked about racism and family and relations between the sexes. And the more I tried to explain what life is like back home, the stranger that country became: a mash-up of flower shows and dog shows and flags and conkers and meat pies and leaking roofs and reality TV shows (I had to explain 'reality') and deportation centres and replacement buses and food-banks and raw sewage on the beaches and donkey rides and foxes sunbathing in suburban gardens and people running marathons dressed as chickens and drunk men in the Tube flailing up a down escalator. I'm sure she thought I was making most of it up, to test her credulity. We keep dogs in our *homes*? We let them sleep on our *beds*? She was fascinated – as if she'd clicked on a random link and found herself on a fetish site. I'm assuming her readers will be told that at Christmas the British knit woolly hats for their dogs.

A man in overalls came out of the door next to us and spoke to the journalist. He was asking if we happened to have a spanner.

I told the journalist that in my country it's not dogs but beggars that are invisible. Or as good as – they are street furniture, and we don't see them. Unless they have dogs with them, in which case we do see them. We don't see the beggars without dogs because eye contact overrides any easy assumption that the beggars themselves are to blame for their condition and opens us up to the possibility that *we* are responsible. Not me personally, but you see the problem? The journalist nodded. She had stopped taking notes and was looking at her watch. Was she running late for another interview? But she needed to know this. We *are* responsible, and we resent the beggars for drumming it in. The dogs are different. We feel sorry for the dogs: they are innocent bystanders caught up in this unholy socio-economic mess just because they are meek and available. By rights they should be chasing sheep in the fields, and we want to make it up to them. We want them to enjoy a couple of lamb chops tonight and we want to feel good about ourselves so we pour some coins into the beggar's cup. But it is in the beggar's interest to keep their dog looking hungry and you can't tell anyone what to do with your charity. I have often given detailed directions to tourists and other lost souls on the street only to see them walk off in completely the wrong direction. Or I have offered my seat on the bus to someone more in need of it and they have said thank you but no, they are getting off at the next stop, and five stops later they are still there, frail and shaking and encumbered but telling me, by refusing to sit down, that I am more in need of a seat than them and I feel – well, it was hard to explain to the journalist exactly what I feel.

Are you getting any writing done, Mike? He tells me he's been rewriting his will. And another list of people he needs to say sorry to. And compiling a playlist for his funeral. And drafting the heartfelt addresses to be read at his memorial service. He is busy.

Mike has cold showers in the morning and sings from Broadway musicals while he's slapping on the lotions. Mike is often late – just ten or fifteen minutes, enough to let everyone know he is worth waiting for. It's a form of flirting. He takes his seniority to myself as a given (be happy, Mike). At night on the balcony he talks about his mother, never his father, and he wears sandals. His toenails are gnarled. I feel a surge of tenderness for his naked, neglected toes.

Mike is not a guy I'd choose to hang out with after school but I have no doubt that if we were strolling along a pier at the seaside and a child fell into the water Mike would immediately dive in to rescue the child. I don't imagine he is a good swimmer and he would get into difficulties himself and have to be rescued, but still. About myself I am less sure.

I want to write about the Scottish woman: how she got here, how she lives, what's on the shelves in her apartment, what keeps her awake at nights, her favourite music, her cure for hiccups, whether the freckles are just on her face and neck or extend over her whole body. Back-story, a love affair: with a student from here who was studying psychology in Glasgow, and she followed him home; or she came to this city on a whim, running from a break-up, and met a fisherman or an engineer or a nightclub bouncer and stayed on. Either way, it didn't work out but she likes it here. Or going back would cost her so much more, emotionally, than it cost her to come here that she's stuck, temporarily, until she works out what she wants to do with her life, but it can become a permanent condition. Or no love angle at all, no back-story – she's just here, a Scotswoman not in Scotland, one of those people who feel more at home the farther away they are from their actual home. But my agent wouldn't like that, she'd want the love interest. Never mind the agent.

I have glimpses, notions, inklings, but no connective tissue.

The sister of the Scottish woman lives in Colorado – divorced, teaches English to immigrants, makes pancakes and quilts.

The mother of the Scottish woman, when making sandwiches, cut off the crusts.

The Scottish woman's freckles are a symptom of a rare skin condition whose cause is unknown. Once, a team of medical researchers wanted to write a paper on her. Fame!

The Scottish woman could give me the lowdown on the dogs.

I know that glimpses and inklings may be all I'll have. And I know that writing has a sly way of being about something different from what it claims to be about, but I want to at least start with the Scottish woman.

As well as his toes, the nakedness and intimacy of Mike's handwriting. Not the flashy flourish he uses when signing on a title page but his crabby little messages on notepaper: rounded letters sloping backwards but the lines themselves sloping up, bunching tightly at the right side of the page. You might see a lack of congruence here between the childishness of his handwriting and the number of characters in his novels who die extravagantly violent deaths but I don't see any contradiction at all.

Wrong place, wrong time – victims who are not the intended victims but who just happen to step into the line of fire. I want to start the day again with them, I want say don't go to work today, phone in sick. Don't catch that bus, wait for the next one. I want to grab their elbow and say don't cross the street now. But it's already too late.

While waiting in the hotel lobby for Mike and Lee I watched four men and two women pacing between the entrance and a potted palm tree, all of them speaking on their phones. Exquisite choreography: one woman turning at the palm tree just as the other reached the doorway, the men on course to collide but avoiding at the last moment with a step to the side. I recognised one of the men who bundled us into a taxi and brought us back from the street market. Burly, muscled: resistance would have been pointless. I nodded to him and he took off his shades but he blanked me.

We assume that our rooms are bugged. Even if our hosts have assumed that we assume that and so haven't bothered, we should feel a little more relaxed when we are sitting outside on Mike's balcony, but this isn't happening. We are failures even at our own double-act.

Mike and I: two sides of the same coin. Heads or tails?

There are writers who are better people than they are writers, and others who are better writers than they are people, and Mike and I tick neither box. We muddle along. Our whole experience here is a train crash in slow motion.

Last night on the balcony I said to Mike that I think I used to write good dialogue, just the right degree of deranged, but now I don't write dialogue at all. I've just become unsociable, Mike suggested.

The guys and girls pacing in the lobby with their mobile phones — sometimes they got out their pocket calculators. They were doing deals. Everyone will get their cut except those who won't. It's how the world tick-tocks: not the press releases but the chitchat in corridors, banter in locker rooms, winks and nods, the nods like those of the always slightly grubby toy dogs I used to see in the back window of the car I was stuck behind in a traffic hold-up on the motorway. Men — almost always — behind closed doors, men scratching each other's backs. The women are in the kitchen, the women are ironing the men's shirts. Men *off the record*. Men on street corners with deep inside pockets, men sitting around low tables in the back rooms of shops that sell a half-bottle of whisky and a packet of dog biscuits per day and that smell of money laundering and bleach. They also operate out of railway arches, crack dens, City wine bars and offices in Whitehall. And badly lit corners of the internet, and brightly lit ones too. They have codes, jargon, nicknames, grudges, tics, scars and bruises and broken noses, some of these men, none of them remarkable on their own but string them together and they become impenetrable. The stakes might be small but day by day and deal by deal these are the strings that bind.

I thought as a child I'd come to know what they were talking about, the men standing on the pavement outside the pub who lowered their voices as I passed by, and that they would let me into their conversation, but they still lower their voices.

A woman once told me that the way to deal with pain was to convince yourself that it is being experienced by someone else. Someone you dislike. You know who. Emotions too – can I offload my anxiety (but keep joy)? I haven't found that this works.

Today at the Writers' Union we were asked our opinion about our own country, and what should or is most likely to happen next. Writers have a lousy track record in making such pronouncements but everyone nodded seriously as we spoke.

We took the metro back to the hotel. Much less staring this time: our novelty value is wearing off. Children were strap-hanging along the length of the carriage, swinging from one hand-hold to the next, laughing as they did so.

Children's mental maps of the world are not more full of holes than those of adults. Different holes.

Two British businessmen tried to talk to us in the hotel bar. They are salesmen for a company that makes security fences and surveillance cameras. One was wearing a Manchester United shirt, the other a Liverpool shirt. Their catalogue has as many endorsements from celebrity dictators as Mike's latest novel has puff quotes from winners of the Booker prize.

Mike asked them, very bluntly, how much they earned and the one in the Liverpool shirt said they mostly worked on commission, and to make any kind of decent money they had to sell and sell and sell. Whether the surveillance cameras actually worked or not. I was about to feel sorry for them but then Mike said it was the same for us writers too. We are all in sales.

The one in the Man United shirt admitted that the cameras they were selling were not all they were cracked up to be. Cheap lenses, fuzzy images. He was inviting intimacy, he was inviting Mike to confide that frankly, his books were a little fuzzy too. And then we could order another round of drinks and have a laugh at the system. But Mike wasn't playing.

We have our differences, Mike and I, but tonight we were united in our resentment of these other Brits. It may not be yielding much fruit but this is our patch.

Mike mentioned again to Lee the postponed visit to the recycling centre and Lee shrugged. He promised to make inquiries. There might be a misunderstanding here, or a mistranslation. Mike's suggestion: a re-education centre? They haven't yet decided whether we are worth recycling or should be sent to landfill.

Shortly after Lee left us in the hotel last night Mike too went out. I heard him coming back at around 4 a.m. Giggles in the corridor: someone was with him. I couldn't sleep. It was too hot in my room and I couldn't turn the heating down.

A thing kings used to do when they distrusted their advisers: exit the palace in disguise at night and wander the streets, to discover what their subjects really thought of them. Or they were just bored by the bowing and scraping and the nursery food and wanted to find what else was on offer. Like children running away. Is this what Mike was doing last night? I doubt it.

When the king got lost he had to ask for directions back to the palace. Across the bridge and then second left, you can't miss it. Everyone knows where the palace is except the king, who has never needed to know.

A woman approached me in the hotel lobby, curious about the attention Mike and I were receiving, and asked: What do you do? I told her we were writers. She was still curious: What *else* do you do?

Presentation: wallpapering.

Next: painting-by-numbers? They are running out of entertainments. They no longer trust us to return home singing the praises of their political system but wallpapering, the world can only stand back and be amazed.

Bin-end, said Mike. He was hungover. His shoelaces were undone. To compensate for his lack of interest, I paid keen attention to the ratio of water to paste when mixing, coverage per kilo of paste, types of brushes . . .

One of the men could have been the twin brother – height, shape of his head, disguised limp – of an English actor in a 1980s sitcom whose name I forget. Reggie? Ronald? Somewhere we all have a double.

Enjoyment from watching a mechanical task being performed in stages – teamwork, efficiency – and relaxing into the rhythm. The kind of job writers are, or used to be, encouraged to have: while the body goes through the motions the mind can work independently, above all this. But mostly the mind just drifts, and when it does snag on something the rhythm of the manual job falls apart and you get sacked.

Suddenly clapping, very loud, it was over. Except not. Everyone was looking at us and grinning: we were expected to step up, Mike and I, and wallpaper. Like politicians serving pints in a pub. They had left a part of the wall for us, a designated section. There was no way out.

Even if we botched it – which we did, getting paste

all over our clothes — they were going to applaud. The whole event was designed to show us that we can do no wrong. Which also means that we can do no right.

Mike: It's the things they are not telling us that we should be paying attention to. As in, you know, *poems*: what's left out is as important as what's put in.

Mike, I get that. I've washed my ears. I'm listening to a lot of silence. We have return tickets.

Or: perhaps there is really nothing more to be known than what we are shown or told, and we are arrogant to believe that there is. Even if there *is* more to know, we don't have a *right* to know it.

Even if we stumble upon more than we are shown or told, that knowledge is useless unless we *do* something with it. Which is why the 'prefer not to know' box gets ticked so often.

The visit to the recycling centre has again been put off. 'Rescheduled.' Both Mike and I now want very much to see the recycling centre. We insist.

Without a language in common with our hosts we are animals sniffing one another's behinds. One smells better than another, but better *how*? Clearly we are being used, we are (very minor) foreign celebrities bought in the marketplace — because we were cheap? Could we have held out for more? – to add a touch of glamour, but our performance is lacking. Our hosts try to hide their disappointment but their own performance falls short too, so at least we are well matched. They have bought a new toy but it turns out to be not as much fun as the picture on the packaging suggests, or the instructions are too complicated. I want to put an arm round their shoulders and say, It's OK, we got off on the wrong foot but we can start again, can't we?

Probably not. Smiles are switched on and then off. We inhabit a buffer zone. Failure to engage.

Failure even to sleep. Sirens, police or ambulance, in the streets. Mike, who has been on a number of these trips, says he can tell which country he is in by the noise the sirens make. The ones here are three-note, with a kind of dip on the third.

Farther away now. Or their batteries are running low.

Mike told me to stop being so wet. He told me to imagine I was *batting for England*.

Adverse reaction in shopping mall. People were staggering under the weight of their boxes and bags – peasants coming home from the fields with the harvest. All too much. I know that's the point of shopping malls, wall-to-wall wish-fulfilment, but all too much of the *same thing*, endlessly repeated, a mirrors game, same as the statistical info we are being spoon-fed on a loop, no way through, and I started to lose the ability to distinguish between the people and the mannequins, between buyers and bought. Everyone was walking at that sludgy pace of the walkways to departure gates in airports which are there so I don't even have to bother putting one foot in front of the other, I can just stand and be transported, raise my arms and surrender, and I asked Lee which boarding gate we were headed to and how much time we had before they closed the gate. Gate number 17, Lee said. And we were in good time. Coffee, go the bathroom, fine. Meanwhile, Mike had found someone else to go shopping with. My eyes hurt; everything was too shiny. I wanted dark glasses and a white stick. I started reciting poetry – it's a defence mechanism – Browning, 'My Last Duchess', and Lee sat me down in a stubby corridor that led to the washrooms and asked me to start again from the top, a little more slowly, don't hurry, take some deep breaths, and he got out his notebook and transcribed. Rapid but very neat handwriting, the rhymes clicking into place. It calmed me.

Where exactly are we? Good question, Mike. Wyoming? The Carolingian Empire? Back in the days. Back in the days. We were younger.

That may in fact have been Mike's question: *When* are we?

At least 80 per cent of the people here are younger than us. Aren't we a bit old to be doing this, Mike? And Mike says: What's the cut-off? He tells me he's fifty-nine. He is starting to worry.

Travels of yesteryear . . . Mind-numbing conversations with other backpackers in flea-ridden hostels about (1) the shallowness of Western materialism and (2) how not to get ripped off in the souvenir shops. My yesteryear self was callow but still right to despise the self who is complaining about the air conditioning in a room he's not even paying for.

I thought it was going to be OK, I thought that being told every day where to go and what to do and not having to make decisions would be a relief, a holiday.

My first dog was a Labrador. He was in place before I arrived. He would disappear for days and then come back, tail wagging. I believed he had two homes, two families, so he wasn't exclusively mine. When he went off to his other family it was my fault for not loving him enough. And when he came back I was overjoyed, he was giving me a second chance. Of course I told that dog things I couldn't tell to any other living being. For the right amount of rump steak that dog could have spilled beans. What happened to him? He was poisoned by some gypsies who camped in a field at the edge of the village and got fed up with him raiding their larder. A likely story, says Mike.

I asked Mike if, when he was at school, he had ever talked with his friends about which was better, dying from being too cold or too hot, and about the best way of killing yourself – bullet or noose, train track or cyanide – and he said of course he had, everyone does. I asked Mike what his nickname was at school and he wouldn't say. I asked Mike if his mother, when making sandwiches, cut off the crusts and he thought for a while and said he couldn't remember. I asked Mike what his favourite colour was and he said grey.

Common cause of death of Englishmen abroad: falling to the pavement from a balcony. High level of alcohol in the blood. Fell or was pushed? The police report is inconclusive.

Not a boarding school, no. A sanatorium. To which the protagonists of the novel have been sent to convalesce. The air is bracing: we are in the mountains, just below the tree line and far from any bus stop. The staff are deferential, the food is five-star, the fees are sky-high (but tax-deductible). Decisions about the patients' medication, and when or if they can be declared 'cured', and when or if they can leave, are entirely up to the director, who wears suits that even Mike couldn't afford and is played by the actor who plays the director of the old folks' home in *Chinatown* – or the director of the rehab place in Altman's *The Long Goodbye*, I may be confusing them, and until my confusion is resolved I won't be let out of here.

The journalist has written up our interview and has sent me the text to approve, in case she has misunderstood anything I told her. It reads like a description of a dystopian country in a bad 19th-century novel. She has informed her readers that all the beggars in my country have been shot and the dogs suffer from Stockholm syndrome. I tell her it's fine. Send it to print.

Sit. Beg. Lie down. Good boy.

Visit to the flagship branch of the state bookshop. Lee was excited, Mike was bemused to discover that there are writers who sell even more books than he does, I was depressed. I didn't even bother writing down the statistics. Mountains of books. Who needs more?

Diary entries and hand-crafted aperçus are fiddling while Rome burns. There is more to be said but most of it – all of it? – has been said before, again and again, and far better than I could ever say it and has made no difference at all.

Story. Or, better, film. Late in life, a critically esteemed and popular comic actor re-watches his career on archive footage and DVDs. Voice-over: plot summaries and memories of behind-the-scenes larks. Location: a mansion-block flat in Mayfair or a room in sheltered housing in the suburbs, it would work either way. The actor was once a household name but if he comes up in casual conversation now the question of whether he is still alive or not is disputed. People make bets on it. Someone googles him on their phone to find out. Someone approaches him in the street in St John's Wood and asks if he's really him and he says no, but he used to be. The actor notices for the first time that every role he has played has an edge of cruelty. This must be part of his enduring appeal.

Diarrhoea. Payback for the day we claimed to be ill and weren't.

I spent the day between bed and toilet. Between lying down and sudden rush. Mid-morning, a knock on the door: I shouted and they went away. But just when I was beginning to think that I was going to die alone, there was another knock and I opened the door: a boy about ten years old, very pale, hair sleeked back, same face he will have when he is forty and running a government department. I let him in. Somewhere in my head the tradition of hospitality to strangers is still embedded, like something my grandmother told me. A tradition now practised only by people in poor countries with the least to share. The boy sat on the end of the bed and bounced up and down, testing the mattress. He tapped the window with his knuckles, calculating how much force would be needed to shatter it. He moved the plant six inches to the left: he is a set designer. I wanted to help him – the plant is heavy – but I was feeling too ill. He inspected the books on the table by the bed, ignored the TV, spent some minutes working out how to close and open the curtains by pulling the cord, talked to me, wasn't in the least bothered that I couldn't understand a word he was saying, then left. To him I was just a another piece of furniture. Mike was out with Lee at a lecture, or watching flower-arranging.

They are so very afraid that we will get lost. (We *are* lost.)

How does the Scottish woman get away with it? Has she paid for a license that permits her to walk the streets without being followed by undercover police? Is *she* being paid, to inform on other foreigners? I assume they have decided that she's harmless and they don't need to keep a constant tab on her, just bring her in every few months to renew her permit.

At some point she may give up on human society. When she is old she will be running a refuge for the

stray dogs that don't exist, and she'll give them names from out of her childhood and tend their open sores. But when the food runs out they will turn on her.

In Vienna in August 1919 Joseph Roth saw a man returned from the war 'in the form of a hinge', with a dog on his back. 'The scene struck me with the force of a revelation: a dog seated on a man. When he remembers what happened when he relied on other men, a man is happy to put his trust in a dog.'

The plant in a pot in my room has bloomed, modestly. It thrives on negligence. Two emergent flowers, one more confident than the other, ivory-ish in colour, an expensive colour, not gaudy. An orchid? I was advised by my grandmother – and I absorbed this widespread belief like a plant absorbs water – that you can have another person in your bedroom, fine, but not a plant because they steal your oxygen while you sleep and you might wake up dead. I am being slowly despatched by flowery means.

Much colder, today.

Small green birds in the bushes in the park, very bright. Pretty. They don't look as if they live here, just passing through on the way to somewhere warmer.

Sexually, nothing doing: shrivelled cock and balls, as if I've been swimming in the North Sea.

Boarded-up windows like eye patches. Also like advertisements: look, there is nobody here.

Lit windows at night advertise human presence. Unless someone has gone for a pee or checked to see if they have left their glasses on the bedside table and forgotten to switch off the light before leaving the room.

Woken this morning by the sound of a dog growling. But there is no dog. A short-haired dog with yellow teeth and electric-blue eyes.

We should be talking not to the people seated next to us at table but to the waiters, the cooks, the kitchen porters, but as Mike points out we don't speak their language and they don't speak ours. He is relaxed about this.

We should be asking what makes them afraid and what, if a genie appeared out of a lamp and granted them three wishes, they would wish for. And not take a shrug for an answer. We shouldn't even need language, we should be able to sense what rings true and what doesn't. Dogs can do this.

The new hydropower plant will have a capacity of 800 MW and will generate 36.7 TWh. Amazing. Applause. I asked about the number of farmers and villagers who will be displaced and Mike kicked me on the shin.

On the balcony later, Mike stubbed out a cigar in the glass he was using as an ashtray and said we are writers and politics is not our job. In front of an audience, if he's feeling expansive he'll say something about literature contributing to the health of society. I think he means *wealth*, not least his own. Writers often get their words a little muddled.

Mike sipped his whisky and gave me a flat stare, daring me to suggest that his was not the last word. He is not a *bad* man. He recycles his waste, he gives up his seat on public transport. He leaves generous tips. He signs petitions to save rainforests and he donates to charities that support writers who have fallen on hard times. I considered picking him up – but Mike is a heavy man – and throwing him off the balcony.

As if he had read my mind, Mike got up from the table and heaved himself onto the balcony wall, doing half my job for me. He sat on the ledge, legs dangling, parading his toes, and asked me to pass him his whisky. I bade him goodnight and went back to my room.

Mike does a lot of nodding. He drapes his arm along the backs of sofas. He drums his fingers. He places his hand on available knees. He is a form of octopus. Octopuses are very intelligent creatures, he tells me; they have nine brains, the main one and then one in each of their tentacles. And they are good at camouflage.

It must be hard to have all that brainpower operating around the clock. Do Mike's arms and legs sometimes come to different conclusions? I've noticed that he has almost no sense of smell.

He treats Lee as if he is our servant. I try to be friendly but when Lee asks us a question it's always Mike he addresses first.

I asked Lee about the Scottish woman, whether he'd ever come across her. He said no, no Scottish woman, and if there was he'd have heard about her. Foreigners are his specialty. But Lee also says there are no dogs.

The thing about taking a nap and a shower and dressing with care before I kill – maybe what's that about is if a thing is worth doing, it's worth doing well. Maybe it's a kind of foreplay, not just etiquette but part of the whole experience, don't rush it. Maybe it's an acknowledgement that killing someone is not like catching a bus, it's more like going to the opera. Maybe it's about respect: it's a dumbed-down secular version of the praise songs hunters sing when they set out on the trail, celebrating the bond between hunter and prey. I don't know, and I don't know anyone I could ask. I could ask Mike.

Mike will tell me that I am overthinking again. Do it spontaneously or not at all. No second thoughts, no first thoughts, no forethought at all. Do it *now*, because it feels right in the moment, even though I know that in the next moment it won't.

The national gallery. I missed the first part of our guide's lecture on contemporary work because I was lingering in an adjoining room that we had been walked through as if it was a store room, nothing of interest here, a room whose walls were stacked with 19th-century genre paintings. The people in these paintings – working in the fields, drinking in taverns, gathered at the bedsides of sick children – were Lee's grandads and grandmums. Two or three generations back, not far at all. One painting showed a funeral procession in the countryside:

priest, acolytes, a horse-drawn cart bearing the coffin and behind it the mourners. I have read this scene in novels, watched it in films. Not this precise cart and coffin but whatever is round the next bend in the road won't come as a surprise.

Genre, always popular, is a way of touching base.

Heavy clouds. Mud. The paint was cracking. Browns and blacks and greys, appropriately bleak. A splash of red on the shawl worn by one of the mourners, third from the left, who was clearly, inarguably, the Scottish woman and this is getting ridiculous.

'It's not for publication, is it?' Mike has discovered that I am writing a journal. He is not worried about the sketches Lee makes in his notebook: 'That's different.' Different how, Mike? He shook his head. We both know how. A flattering sketch by someone who doesn't know you is not the same as appearing in a published book by a writer who you suspect is not 100 per cent a fan of your work. I assured Mike that I am not writing for publication. But still, Mike said, if I become successful, a writer on the syllabus, someone will dig it out and add an intro and footnotes and send it to print.

Most writers harbour a fantasy that one day they will sell a million copies, don't they? Royalties! Reprints! Queues for signing at festivals! *National treasures!* They don't usually admit it. Their partners tease them about it.

I laughed but Mike didn't. Unlikely, I said. And anyway, we'll both be dead by then.

I don't think the possibility that he might die had occurred to Mike. People die in novels but that's not the same.

But if not for publication, why?

Dizziness. Light-headed when I stand up, lack of balance. Carbon monoxide poisoning? Not rabies: I am not hallucinating, I am not vomiting, there are no stray dogs. Lee has brought me some pills that look like throat lozenges. To suck or swallow? I haven't taken them. Nor have I thrown them away.

Mike is not affected. He has been spending more nights out, playing truant, not coming back to the hotel until the small hours. Often he is with a woman; sometimes I hear them and sometimes not but their perfume is still there in the corridor in the morning. We are not just ambassadors on public show, we have private lives too, but there's not much privacy in a hotel.

Sex is a part of what hotels are for. The cleaning ladies in the corridors give me sorrowful looks.

I have written a letter of complaint to the hotel management about the air conditioning. First, it is very loud: less a hum than a *buzz*. Can you dial it down? But I can live with that. More especially: during the day it's too cold and at night it's so hot I can't sleep, and this is not good for my health. It cannot be good for the plant too, which now has half a dozen flowers but they all look sickly. When I click the button on the control panel to adjust the temperature nothing happens. Stand-off. It is one of those buttons that don't actually connect to anything, it's there to give me the *illusion* of agency. I admit that this is sometimes enough, and that having control over every aspect of my life all my waking hours would be scary, but wanting a good night's sleep is not asking for much, surely? It cannot be difficult.

In the letter I mentioned my childhood asthma and my hay fever too, and the days in summer when the pollen count was high and I had to stay indoors while the others played outside, and how these medical conditions led to my being perceived as a loner, a perception that may or may not have contributed to my becoming a writer. I didn't make a big deal of this. I wasn't claiming that people who are good at sport cannot also be writers. I wasn't asking for sympathy, just a decent temperature in my room.

Calm, reasonable tone, but firm. Every sentence earned its place, good rhythm. It's the best thing I've written for months. I am not expecting a reply.

I asked Mike where he gets his limitless supply of cigars from and he winked. A wink is worse than a nod, worse than a shrug, a wink is sneaky. I refuse to be a conspirator. Yesterday one of the hotel cleaning women winked at me in the corridor, I have no idea why. I turned to see if she was winking at someone behind me but no, nobody.

Heard from the balcony, a dog howling. Mike was drunk. Mike howling? A wolf? There are no dogs.

Stray dogs adapt over time to their habitat and acquire a basic set of survival skills. They travel in from the suburbs to the centre of town, where the food is better, on the metro or tram. They cross streets at the traffic lights. They know how to beg, they know about eye contact. Within a few generations they will be swapping recipes and booking holidays online and checking their investment portfolios. They *learn*, because they have to, while reserving the right to froth at the mouth and bite off your fingers without warning. This is their city too.

Also stray people. I mean people not loved by other people.

Linking hands, a man and a woman ran across a street just as the lights changed and the traffic started up. Applauded by an angry blare of car horns, they arrived at the kerb on the high of having cheated death by inches.

The thrill, and embarrassment, of *getting away with it*.

I want to go home.

Today, as I was slurping my breakfast gruel in the hotel dining room, I experienced a déjà-vu, my first for many years. Over by the entrance to the room, Mike appeared with a woman dressed for something more grand than a hotel breakfast, hand in hand, and there was a moment when they were walking past the faux palm tree and Mike bent his head to whisper something into her ear when I knew I had been here before, had seen Mike and that woman in that exact position, a waitress passing behind them exactly then, the light in the room exactly so, even though this was impossible because I had never seen that woman in my life.

She turned out to be an archaeologist, very friendly and far more informative than any of our official guides. Many rings on slender fingers; healthy appetite.

I asked her about the dogs and she said that during the cull a pack of them had escaped to the mountains, where they are demanding recognition of an independent state. She smiled warmly and placed her hand on my wrist to reassure me. The mountains are very far away.

Someone slipped an envelope under the door of my room. Inside there was a handwritten note: 'Thursday 9 meat cellar. Green dress.' Then a couple of Xs for kisses and an initial: L. Or maybe it was a C. In fact all the handwriting was ambiguous: 'meet caller'? I assumed a confusion of doors and this was for Mike from one of his women but when I showed it to him he said it was a ransom note: 'We have your dog. Send us a million dollars or your dog will die.' When I showed it to Lee he laughed and tore it up.

The plant with its sickly flowers is at least making an effort. I feel more kindly towards it. It occurred to me that maybe my room really is bugged, and that somewhere concealed within the plant is a tiny microphone, and the plant's flowers were its way of apologising for spying on me. I began looking for the microphone but succeeded only in cutting my finger on one of the leaves: two bright beads of blood, like the flecks of blood when my tooth fell out. The blood also reminded me of the splash of red on the shawl of the Scottish woman in the painting of the funeral. And how the missing button on the shirt of the boy who was reciting a poem rhymed with the missing stanza. There is safety in rhyme: rhymes say that life adheres to a pattern, and things are meant to be as they are. This is a lie but it's a seductive one.

Clarity. Exhilaration. Mike slipped on the steps as we were coming out of the Museum of Eschatology, let go of the bundle of paper he was carrying, which happened to be the proofs of his new book, and a spirited but fierce gust of wind edited them, scattering the pages and sending them high and far. Everything up in the air – hats, gloves, wigs, scarves, passwords, secrets, lies, truths, everything we thought we had hold of, characterisation and structure the least of it – and people were rushing around, bumping into each other and gleefully snatching what pages they could and bringing them back to Mike. A prize, surely, for the most pages saved? A signed copy of the first edition. Mike sat on the next-to-bottom step – he had twisted his ankle – with his head down: his carefully constructed plot had exploded.

Or perhaps he hadn't slipped – he had simply thrown up his hands. Joy of *letting go*.

They were only page proofs, I told Mike. We were on the balcony. He was blowing this up, conflating it with all his other troubles, he was quoting Freud, 'What do women want?' Mike, let's start with: 'What did Freud want?' The original file must still be somewhere. The proofs can be printed out again or sent as a pdf. The plot still hangs together, doesn't it? No inconsistencies, no pot-holes, the road running smooth, everything filled in.

Mike went into the bedroom to get more whisky and trod a chocolate liqueur into the carpet, or a snail or an eyeball. Tough job for the cleaning ladies.

I found Mike in the hotel bar with the salesmen peddling surveillance hardware and the man I mistook in the lift for Harry and his companion who wanted to scare me off. She smiled at me, made room on the sofa and patted the space beside her. They were being merry. On their third or fourth bottle. I gave my room number to the woman behind the bar but she said no one was staying there and refused to serve me.

Mike was in a wheelchair. His twisted ankle. Women will mother him. He is rehearsing his role as Grand Old Man. Is there still some mileage in that?

I went back to my room and dozed off and dreamt I was at a fairground shooting gallery, holding an air rifle. The targets, fixed to a chain that moved jerkily across the back of the gallery, were cut-out figures of famous dictators who all looked like first cousins of Mike. They send one another Christmas cards. If I hit three I won a goldfish in a bag of water. It looked easy but the barrel of the gun was skewed.

King Lear: 'The little dogs and all, / Tray, Blanch, and Sweetheart, see, they bark at me.'

The dogs are here, of course. It's just that, as with the name of God in certain religions, we are forbidden to speak their names.

Small, pocket-sized items have been disappearing from my room, things of no account: socks, a hairbrush, a pen. Not the pen I've had for decades, the writer's fetish object, the one that outlasts marriages even though it doesn't actually write very well, but the spare one I used at the book fair when I was signing copies of whichever book was thrust into my hands and which may have just fallen out of my pocket.

I wouldn't even notice these things were gone unless I looked for them – so I must be missing other things too, things I haven't looked for because I didn't even know they were gone, big things as well as little ones, things with capital letters like Justice and Love, things so big I took it for granted they were always there.

A photograph from my wallet. This shouldn't matter but it does. Can people steal a memory?

I am being *chipped away at* and I think Mike feels this too, and this isn't good for our relationship. Not that there was much there to begin with. We are simple animals and in theory need just one shared interest to believe we have an intimate bond. Jazz, or football, or an elderly relative who needs looking after. But in our case, the fact that we are both scribblers seems to set us apart.

An olive branch: I apologised to Mike for being so peevish. It's because I am disappointed in *myself*. It's because I don't really know what I am doing here and the weather is bad and we are confined to barracks and I feel I am being punished but I don't know what I've done wrong and we are being treated like elderly celebrities by people who struggle to remember what we were famous for and so, often, do we. It may not be worth remembering anyway. Whatever it was, it changed nothing.

Bollocks, Mike said. The reason I'm tetchy is that I'm not getting laid, simple as that. He may be right. The prospect is bleak.

Even if they come back — the socks, the hairbrush, the pen, the memory — and some of them do, restored to where they belong — they are tainted now, as if while away they have been *turned*. Should I hire a lawyer?

The numbers are slipping away too, slipping off the map. I'm not sorry. At the start of this trip I wrote down the facts and figures they told us; it would have been disrespectful not to. The point of all those grain harvests and tons of concrete was to convince us that everything was nailed down and under control. To be able to admit that it never was is a relief.

Much collar-scratching from Lee when I asked if we could throw a wild party and invite all the cleaning ladies and their families and the secret policemen too.

In a park, groups of men and women of all ages in *leisure-wear*, doing gymnastic exercises, perfectly co-ordinated, swinging their arms and bending, as if they were scything the grass.

I pointed to a dog taking a dump next to a waste bin. Lee said he saw no dog. I approached, warily, and the dog growled at me and finished its business and turned tail. No dog, said Lee, smiling, despite the steaming evidence on the ground in front of us.

And then Mike, echoing Lee, also said no dog. No wink this time, he was deadpan, this man who perceives the whole world as a practical joke so he might as well join in. Or perhaps he really does not see what I am seeing. If people sell you a line for long enough – or you sell it to yourself – then you do come to believe it.

Mike's wheelchair has gone but he carries a stick – to ward things off or point to the extent of his domain. Sometimes he wields it like a cricket bat, playing a shot through the covers. Lee is puzzled.

Seen again, the three-legged dog: scruffy white, mongrel, not big, one ear torn and blind in one eye. Male or female, I have no idea. Today was the third or fourth sighting: this dog is following me around, is becoming my familiar. Is it trying to tell me something? I bent down, getting close and smelly, and whispered to this dog – but it probably knew this already, and it may well be deaf as well as half-blind – that many of my perfectly well-sighted fellow humans *choose* to turn a blind eye to what is going on in the world. It wagged its tail. Gallows humour. It is on its way out, it hasn't got much time left, but still, I should give it a name.

Last night on the balcony Mike asked me if I ever thought I had *missed the boat*.

New woman at the reception desk in the hotel: brilliant white teeth – shrill.

Feeling of mild sexual excitement in the lift going up. Same as in the lift at the college of engineering a few days ago. Does this only happen when the lift is going up? Do other men feel this? Do women? Opposite effect when the lift is going down?

The black dog, circling. Somewhere between three and six in the afternoon, neutral light filtered through unwashed windows – too late, too early – a chronic low-level sense of waste, and small hope that the evening will redeem that.

Traffic slides by, keeping in lane, everyone waiting their turn, not drowning but not waving either.

On an afternoon in 1320, say, a woman weaving cloth on a rooftop looks up from her work and sees a dust cloud on the horizon under a sky that is almost pure white. Goats, and two goatherds – brothers, the sons of her cousin. But one of these days it will be the barbarians, and by midnight the city will be on fire . . .

Bang bang bang – staccato barrage – gunshots? Not far away, no more than a couple of streets. Or fireworks? No guns, Lee will say.

Mike's ankle has healed. He has dispensed with his stick. He kept leaving it behind and people kept bringing it back to him, thinking they were doing him a favour.

Essay: the pressure of nothing happening. Agent, are you there? Is anyone?

Once upon a time, when I was very small and the grass was green, I saw a waitress deliberately let drop to the floor a whole tray of food and drink. Why I remember this is because I still feel responsible, it was my fault. She was sacked, I assume. And if this was a 19th-century novel, which on the whole it still is, her only available next move was to sell sex on the streets.

'The whole cloud of nothing in particular that wraps around us each day, inside and outside the hotel, indescribable.' Celati.

Dear [*illegible*] – This morning, out of the car window, I saw a woman on the pavement being hit with sticks by three men. Repeatedly. Batons, not sticks: polished and heavy and wielded by men in uniform and designed for clubbing people not in uniform. I used to think of these as ornamental, not functional. I have led a sheltered life. I felt pathetically happy that the woman was not red-haired. A few pedestrians had stopped to watch but most were walking by as if a woman being beaten to a pulp, or a man, or a dog, was no more worthy of notice than an apple spilling from a shopping bag. Up ahead the road appeared to be blocked and Lee spoke angrily to our driver. The driver was big and the car was small but it was *his*, he had worked every hour of the day for many years to acquire this car and he didn't like people shouting in it so he shouted back. For a moment I believed that Lee and the driver were about to exchange blows, that the violence I had witnessed outside the car was about to be replicated *inside* the car – that in fact the beating of the woman could not end until this had happened – and there would be blood on the seats, teeth even, but then the driver shrugged, perhaps because he had decided there would be no pleasure in hitting a man so much smaller than himself, perhaps because he couldn't afford to lose this fare and this job, and he reversed and turned the car and we drove back to the hotel in silence. Lee stared hard at me and shook his head – not to express sorrow but to tell me I hadn't seen what I had seen. No dogs, no woman and no men wielding batons. Mike too claims that he saw nothing, he was *reading some poems* a student had sent him. I need to tell you this – there is no one else – or it will be as if there really had been nothing to see. Meanwhile, in assembly rooms and lecture halls we are wrapped in a blanket of 'solidarity' and 'progress' – language-laundering. Take care, please, in this careless world. I feel very far away.

Homesickness. For my own bed, obviously. And for [*illegible*]'s bed. House keys digging a hole in my pocket. Ironing shirts on Sunday evenings. Putting out the rubbish. Pale brown envelopes through the letter flap. Dripping tap in the kitchen, deal with it tomorrow. No one staring at me on buses and trains. Special offers: bacon roll for £2.99 with any hot drink before 11 a.m., and the man trudging down the Uxbridge Road in the rain with a sandwich board promising eternal life who looks so forlorn I want to hug him. The dog-eared notices thumb-tacked to trees with photos of missing dogs: 'Reward offered'. The dogs have been stolen and sold on.

A woman returns to the city after many years away and shows strangers in the street, in cafés and buses and shops, a crumpled photograph of a handsome and disarmingly young man in uniform. People look closely at this photograph, afraid to touch it with their fingers because every handling will make it more fragile but they really do want to help, they want to be part of this story and they want it to have a happy ending; then shake their heads and say, 'I'm not from here.'

Since witnessing the woman being clubbed on the pavement I keep seeing people with bruises and scars and imagining where and how they got them. After the first blow the others follow on fast. And thinking of the lies people tell the doctor: I fell out of bed, I slipped, I walked into a plate-glass door.

Outside the door of the hotel, in that space where taxis draw up and we wait for our car, Mike and the archaeologist were having a kind of tug of war – he was trying to pull her into the hotel, she was trying to pull him out into the street. Neither would let go. I didn't want to watch this – no: I didn't want Mike to catch me watching – so I turned away and there at the far end of the lobby was the taxi driver who had driven us back from the incident with the batons. He was sitting with three other men, also drivers; it is rare to see taxi drivers standing up. Traffic fumes, long hours, sallow skin. Shop talk: road closures, battery life, best products for cleaning urine, vomit, semen and blood from the seats. Sticky is OK, if you have the right product – they don't come cheap – but you don't want to leave them until they get crusty.

I have seen that film about a comic actor revisiting his old films, I now remember. Or part of it. I had come home late and alone and drunk and had turned on the TV and started channel-hopping and I got stuck on an ageing actor watching one of his early sketches and finding it distinctly unfunny, though I myself was joining in with the canned laughter in the original recording. I remember speaking aloud to the TV screen, telling the actor to lighten up and stop being so hard on himself. At this stage there are very few stories I haven't read or seen snatches of at 3 a.m. in the morning.

This morning Mike told me that when he came in last night he found me asleep on his balcony – 'passed out' – with an empty bottle of whisky next to my chair. He says he had to call room service and get help to carry me to my bed, and while they were doing this I woke up and started shouting. What was I shouting? Mike did the national shrug, as if born to it. Is he one of us or one of them? Just shouting, he said. Nothing intimate, I didn't give away any secrets. I was relieved. And disappointed: if I don't have any secrets, what have I been doing with my life?

I have a bruise on my left thigh, just below the hip, but no memory of what caused it. I feel fine, no hangover, not even dizzy. In fact everything appears today as if it has been *rinsed*, with great clarity.

Deleted scenes. *Deletions*: a book made up entirely of deleted scenes? Agent: 'There is usually a good reason *why* they have been deleted.'

Mike in his dressing gown and sandals in mid-morning on the balcony of his hotel room. A fine red velvet dressing gown, though with a number of small holes made by ash falling from his lit cigars. A chambermaid in the doorway to the balcony is offering to mend the dressing gown but Mike doesn't understand what she is saying (he cannot read the subtitles). She repeats her offer, louder, thinking he may be deaf.

Chambermaid opens bedside drawer in Mike's room and finds the dog's foot that Mike took from the stall in the street market. She screams.

Lee on a scooter, weaving through busy traffic. Noise, dust, shouts, movement, music from the cars. Siren blaring, an ambulance passes by in the opposite direction. Lee stops at a red light; among the pedestrians crossing the street in front of him is the Scottish woman.

Through the closed glass door of an office, Lee (standing) is seen arguing with a man seated behind a desk. On the wall is a framed photo of a fat-cheeked man in military uniform. On the desk, an ashtray filled with stubbed-out cigarettes.

A man throws a stone at a dog to scare it off. The dog chases the stone, as it might chase a ball thrown by its owner in a park, and is confused by the man throwing a second stone before it has returned the first one. The dog barks while dodging the stones, getting closer to the man each time he has to pause to pick up another.

Scottish woman at a basin in a bathroom, cleaning her teeth, spitting. Mike on the toilet, trousers down, waving to camera.

Hard rain on the hotel balcony at night. Flooded ashtray, smashed whisky glass. Dog under the table, wet and shivering. Dog gets up and paws at the door of Mike's room, pleading to be let in.

Panoramic views of the city from the hotel balcony in various weathers, at various times of day. Moors in Yorkshire, in sunshine after rain. Fillers.

Someone very famous was imprisoned in this room, the guide told us, and now look at the state of it. He asked us to count the buckets placed under leaks in the roof. I counted six and the guide said there were eight. What were we supposed to do – get out our chequebooks on the spot? Or did he have a card reader?

Further down the street was a shop selling second-hand miracles. And another selling second-hand nooses.

My finely crafted letter of complaint about the air conditioning – a submission to the editor – has been rejected. No right of appeal.

Too late anyway. Yesterday the air conditioning shut

down. No hum, no buzz. In the sudden silence, a feeling of weightlessness, as if I was falling down a lift shaft but had time to spare.

Lines of soldiers standing to attention. It is a still photo except for the movement of the leaves of the tree, upper right, ruffled by a breeze.

People in the street rarely look *up*. Snipers know this.

The statue of the Great Embezzler. The statue of the Assassins. The statue of Discount, sometimes confused with the statue of the Loss Leader. The statue of Diminished Responsibility. The statue of Mary-Jane. The statue of Some Guy Smoking a Cigar. The statue of Glut. The statue of Sub-prime Derivatives. The statue of Reverse Cowboy. The statue of Nominal Reparation. The statue of Sublimated Shit. The statue of the Unknown Dog.

Lee showed us a photo of his wife and son that he keeps in his wallet. His wife is slim and dark and looks too young to be the mother of a teenage boy. Their son is expressionless, not just giving nothing away but refusing even to admit there is anything to give. In the background, a yard with a tin bucket and a stumpy tree. I asked where the photo was taken and Lee told us that he was born and grew up in the countryside, in a village by a lake. I'm seeing hills, valleys, *gorges*, and waterfalls and caves and rocky precipices, a whole Romantic panorama but I can taste the poverty.

Then he showed us a map on his phone. A yellowing page in an old school atlas would have made more sense.

He told us a long story about a frog, a fish and a dog and when he got to the end he laughed and I realised it was a joke but I didn't get it.

His grandmother used to tell him that story, he told us, while she was cooking frogs, a good source of protein. And he mentioned that as a child he stammered – that's why he learned English, that's why he pushed himself into a job that required speaking in public.

So Lee is a performance artist too. He stopped talking and we looked at each other in silence. He was gripping his yellow beret in his lap and turning it around, as if searching for a different wavelength. His bitten fingernails.

The damp patch on the carpet in my room has returned. Near but not in the same place as before. Playing hard to get. Even if this one dries out I will now be expecting another. These things come in threes – like buses and suitors and Goldilocks' bears and Lear's daughters and his dogs too. And then there will be some kind of resolution and we can all go home. I am not averse to happy endings. I reported the damp patch to the shrill-toothed woman at reception and she said she would *log* it. I could write another letter to the editor but by now I understand there is no editor, there is only hot-desking.

On the wall behind the reception desk there are four clocks, showing the time in cities in different times zones around the world. I pointed out that the London one appeared to have stopped – it is still showing the same time as it did when we arrived. The woman smiled and thanked me for pointing this out. End of conversation.

Bunches of cut flowers tied to railings and lamp posts or on the pavements, propped up against a wall. Fresh for less than an hour, spoiled by traffic fumes. The gesture is surely universal: they commemorate bicyclists or pedestrians killed in traffic accidents. I am sad about the lost life but I feel sorry for the flowers too, wilting under the burden of their symbolic weight. Did I simply not notice them before, or are there suddenly a lot more of them?

Also more helicopters. I assume they are searching for fugitives but Mike says they are a new tourist attraction, the city seen from above with a bottle of champagne. They are both: the police funded by tourism. Their noise is an angry headache. Their blades are drilling holes in the sky; soon there will be so many holes that the sky will collapse.

Since Lee refused to recognise the existence of the dog doing a crap in the car park, I've been seeing more of them too. Dogs of all shapes, sizes and breeds. I'm finding it hard to pay attention to what's in front of me because I keep getting distracted by movement to the side, one dog and then another.

There is a reason dogs go blind: they have seen enough.

A rare message from my agent: I am not at a house-party in the Cotswolds but still, I am in a holed-up situation here with a limited cast of characters cut off from the outside world and it's a classic scenario – surely I can contrive a murder mystery out of this? She dangles potential sales figures. This is a very good idea. I'll work on it.

Today Mike told me – why? Intimations of mortality? – that in some cultures when you die they dispose of your body as fast as they can but in other cultures they wait weeks, months, before the burying or the burning because they believe there's a period – a dimension, let's say: he found it hard to be specific about this – between dying and death. I asked Mike which he'd prefer and he replied that it's not up to him but if pressed he'd choose the former. No need to drag things out.

Dream. I am in the fitness centre in the basement of the hotel, among the rowing machines and the exercise bikes and the treadmills, alone, but I am not alone because there are dogs here too. Scores of them. Milky

eyes and puss oozing from open sores. Some are skeletal corpses on the polished black floor and some are so weak they can hardly stand but others are prowling and they haven't eaten for a very long time. Lights are flashing on the exercise machines. Loud music — not the disco stuff but something ecclesiastical, played on an organ by a boy I knew in school, a prodigy. He died young. I try to stay very still. But the dogs can smell me, I know that, and I know the doors are locked, and I am meat.

Rumours . . . The dogs in the mountains, that one again, but now they are preparing for an assault on the city. Dogs are being smuggled down from the mountains and onto the plains in white vans. Leaflets are being dropped from the air in the western suburbs demanding that citizens lay down their arms and surrender (to who?). The president is negotiating over land rights. The president has fled to Mongolia with his son, the one for whom the winning tickets in the national lottery were reserved. The president's second son has defected to the dogs. The water supply has been contaminated. A plane is being sent to evacuate us. We are being held hostage and will be used to bargain for the release of prisoners. Neither of the last two seem plausible: we are simply not that important.

We may be here for months. Along with many others, we may die here. I mentioned this to Mike and he said that we will cross that bridge when we come to it. And after a pause he said it doesn't really matter *where* we die, does it?

Presentation: butchery. Homework: formulae for calculating the surface area of a person.

Nothing on TV except cookery programmes and wildlife documentaries. Gazelles and wildebeest cascading across a dusty plain, close-ups of leopards looking heroic and bored: better than a blank screen with martial music. I muted the volume. Leave the soundtrack to the animals: yelps, grunts, gnawing of bones. Pawing of ground, scratching. Silence. They are supernaturally – I mean naturally, but by now we accept any kind of stage-managed rendition of reality as 'natural' – beautiful, and so efficient in what they're cut out to do, a lot of which is killing.

Again the room is too hot, even without the air conditioning. I switch channels, trying to find a documentary made in the Arctic.

As casually as I switch channels, someone has changed genres while I wasn't looking. Before, at least we used to know roughly what was expected of us; now we feel miscast and under-rehearsed.

After a while – not long at all – men walking around car parks with sub-machine guns appear completely normal.

I'm guessing that first-time astronauts are excited by weightlessness – *Look, I can fly!* – and after just a few hours it becomes nothing to write home about.

Hot springs. Geysers. Fishing villages. Wine festivals, dance festivals. Beauty contests, even. I'd like there to be these for us to be taken to, but if there are they have been keeping them quiet.

Instead, we were taken to see an unfinished overhead motorway that will halve the time it takes to get from the airport to the centre of town. When they told us that its construction has already taken over twice as long as originally planned, and has cost more than three times the original estimate, I understood that the whole thing was a joke – a joke of the kind I often don't get but still laugh at the point where I think I'm supposed to laugh because if I don't someone will have to explain the joke and they will resent me for that.

We climbed a ladder. For Mike this wasn't easy. He didn't want any photographs but he needn't have worried, they have stopped taking photos. We stood in the rain on a platform that swayed in the wind, and no one could hear the speeches. We looked at a concrete flyover like a giant torso whose arms have been amputated. We weren't dressed for this.

As we were about to climb down a bird flew into me. I screamed but it was more a shriek of laughter than of pain – the joke was on me. It wasn't just that the bird didn't see me, it was if I *wasn't there*. Like the dogs.

A glancing blow but Lee was worried by the blood on my cheek – or by my laughter, which always confuses him – and wanted to take me to a hospital. I refused. We came back to the hotel and with the help of the archaeologist woman with long fingers who happened to be waiting in the lobby, and who was very kind, I patched myself up. I think Mike was jealous: why didn't the bird fly into *him*? For men, bandages are status symbols: you have been in a fight.

And then . . . Mike went out last night and came back alone, very late, knocked on my door, stood at the end of my bed and said he was sorry, he had told me a lie, he is not fifty-nine, he is sixty-two. He has checked his passport. He was sopping wet from the rain. I'm sorry, Mike, but you have woken me up just to tell me how old you are? Do you want me to say you look young for your age? Do you want me to tell you it's *not too late*? Because if so, you need to go and wake up someone else.

Then he mumbled something and I asked him to speak up and he asked if he could dedicate his next book to me. Of course there is a *next* book, but this came out of the blue. He had prepared a little speech. I did him the courtesy of propping myself up on a pillow. He said he admired my writing, he said he respected my 'integrity', he said he had been dealing with some stressful issues and that my companionship during this trip had helped him very much. This frightened me, a little: Mike had been hacked into. Water was dripping off his coat onto the carpet. He appeared to be quite sober. I wanted him to be drunk, so that neither of us need remember this in the morning. I told him to sit down and he said he preferred to stand. At least get a towel from the bathroom and dry his hair? He did that, then didn't know what to do with the towel. He draped it over the plant. Mike, there are flowers on that plant now, do you not see *anything*? They need to breathe. His hair was tousled and my hairbrush wasn't where I told him to look for it. A boy summomed to the head teacher's study – he held his passport in his hand like a sick-note from his mother. Mike, I know all that blustering confidence is just an act, we all have an act, and that it must be exhausting and that deep down you are just as fucked-up as the rest of us and you are trying to deal with this but it's three in the morning and I have been assaulted by a bird and I am tired too, Mike, I am *very* tired, and can't this wait till tomorrow? OK, fine, dedicate your next bestseller to me, thank you. I love you too. Now just let me go back to sleep.

For three days we have not been outside the hotel. Cue the Resurrection? Rushing around has been replaced by waiting. Same difference: we never really knew where we were rushing to, and now we don't know what we are waiting for.

Lee arrives later each day. Punctuality, which was

always a substitute for something else – the lecture was pointless but we scored points for arriving on time – is fraying. Lee's voice is also fraying: the stammer he had as a child has returned. We tell him we want to go to the central market and he shrugs and gestures to the window: rain, still rain. His words are running out. He has stopped fussing about brushing dog hairs from his clothes and about this I am glad.

Rain: to begin with it is personal but the longer it goes on the more it becomes just a fact of life.

The archaeologist woman called by with cigars and a bottle of black-market whisky for Mike, and to ask how the cut on my face is healing. Her range of expertise is impressive. She told us about the quality of the food in prisons. And about dogs not being worried by any fancy notions of democracy – they are pack animals, they are interested only in their place in the pecking order. And about what male writers reveal about themselves when they write about women. When I suggested that men tend to hold grudges while women are more forgiving she told me not to be too sure about that.

Back in my room, I turned on the tap in the basin and it spat, gargled and spluttered before emitting a gush of brownish, brackish water.

The performance of luxury is over. It was always a finite resource. No one is cleaning our rooms. Mine smells not of air freshener but of *me*: clothes scattered, smears on the bathroom mirror, the bed sweaty and crumpled.

Dust is not residue, dust is a life-form, proliferating, second cousin of algae and moss.

We fall asleep amid the sweet, cloying perfume of a city breaking apart.

We don't need to go out. Sirens, heaps of uncollected refuse, smouldering fires: a standard news-channel aesthetic. Looting. Vigilantes. Power cuts – the hotel will organise games of murder-in-the-dark. Been there, going there again, a gravitational pull. The difference is that this time we are *inside* the TV screen. A child on the beach spends all morning making a sandcastle, eats half of a sandwich, gets bored, then takes a run-up and obliterates the castle with one jump. Guilty Pleasures: essay? Agent, you will like that title. The look on the boy's face as he hits the sand is the glee of revenge – on his better self? On the gritty sandwich? Meanwhile, in the lowlands, drivers slow down as they pass a car crash on the motorway, rubbernecking, then get home safely, park neatly in the driveway and log on or tune in to dis-aster-porn, entropy's highlights. Achievement is sus-pect. Happiness is intolerable. Are we going to the dogs because that's the only way to go or because we expect to? Is there something genetic in this? Agent, are you still there?

Who will win the book prize? The entrails of slaughtered animals are examined by a committee of diviners. I'm watching their body language. I suspect a stitch-up.

I cried this morning. No reason. I wasn't sad, angry, happy, relieved, nothing of those. I felt my eyes watering and put my hands up to my cheeks and they were wet. I took this as a good omen.

Aged sixteen, the Scottish woman was waiting at a bus stop one evening and when the bus arrived she could see the reflection in the bus's windows of everyone in the queue except herself and she knew had already left.

Body aches, mind is shredded. Not just the socks and the hairbrush but names and dates are going missing, the basic coordinates. I look for a comb or a bottle-opener and I can't even remember the *shape* of what I am looking for. In order not to forget it I have given the name of my agent, Lucy, to the three-legged dog.

We blunder about the world, Mike and I, worrying that we've not washed behind our ears, flinching at cockroaches in the shower, signing copies of our books for strangers, making a mess for others to clear up. But the exercise is good for us, Mike says. It's not healthy, sitting at a desk all day.

And then as he leaves the room to answer an urgent call – agent? Lover? Fraud department of his bank? – he does a little skip, showing off his perfectly fit, unsprained ankle. Accompanied by a smirk. He knew that crunch-time was coming. His BMW is part of a set and though he hasn't got the full collection – off-shore trust fund, private jet, well-stocked bunker – he's been banking on this, grab stuff while you can, a perfectly rational response to the shortness of life.

He thinks I knew it was coming too, he reckons he knows me better than I know myself, and he might be right, though whether he's right or not is of no importance. He had a wobble on the night when he asked if he could dedicate his book to me but my *integrity* as he put it is no threat to him at all.

The carpets in the hotel corridors are patterned with brown and blue swirls and they are the same on every floor, which is why it took me some time to realise that I had exited the lift too soon. Shipwreck, this pattern is called. I ploughed on, through the swirls, becoming gradually more sea-sick and putting so much effort into dismissing from my mind the clichés of what was going on in the rooms behind each door I was passing – run-of-the-mill sex, emotional torture, sad wanks to adult-channel porn, re- and re-reading the room-service menu as if this was an Early Renaissance poem — that I didn't notice that the numbers on the doors were wrong until I saw, sitting outside room 907, standing in for a pair of shoes — which will wait in vain to be taken down to the basement and polished — the three-legged dog. Lucy. We looked at each other, without surprise. With a neighbourly respect for each other's privacy. Front left leg the one missing, in case I haven't specified before. *Sorry*, I said, *wrong floor*, and turned back towards the lift.

Coming out of the lift on the top floor, I found Mike teaching Lee to play cricket in the corridor outside our rooms. There are rules: if the ball hits another guest's door the batter is out, caught. If the ball runs all the way to the end of the corridor it's a four.

I still have options. I could turn state informer. (Unlikely. The state already knows far more than I do.) Retrain as a pizza chef. I could get hold of a gun — ask the woman at reception. Not Lee, who would say 'No guns!' and is incorruptible, but there's bound to be *someone* who will sell me one. I could chase after the Scottish woman and be humiliated. I could read an anthology of Jacobean drama: gratuitous violence with heartstoppingly beautiful lines. I could make a run for it. (Where to?)

Sometimes I choose one thing at random, simply to get the other things out of my head. I know that any decision commits me to others — just as this sentence requires a next one, not to be left exposed — but the option of turning my face to the wall, and making that the last one, I'm not ready for that, yet, or not up to it.

This morning when I woke I reached out my hand and you were not there. I don't know the way home.

Like weightlessness, terror can become the norm. But I don't feel stressed. This is not a job interview.

We sat in the lobby with a pack of cards and Mike explained the rules of poker. I think everyone knew them already. The shrill woman joined us. Lee bluffed like a pro and kept winning, raking in our last dollars.

'No one remembers the freckles.' But *I* do. I remember the freckles.

Or the city has emptied out — as in high summer, when the inhabitants flee to the mountains or the coast, leaving behind closed shutters and traffic lights blinking to no traffic at dusty crossroads. Trees doze. Fountains are parched. Phones ring dead. Emails are set to auto-reply. In the foyers of banks security guards recite the epic poems of their ancestors to empty water coolers. Don't die now, a usually taciturn boy tells the woman who suffers a heart attack while climbing the stairs to the sixth floor because the lift is kaput: wait until the holidays are over, when there'll be people around to bury you. Strangers take hold of her elbows, very gently, and she knows that her life is no longer her own. The balding man in the newspaper kiosk has made a pillow of his folded arms; to buy cigarettes you have first to ring a bell to interrupt his humdrum dreams. Foreign students too poor to leave the city lie on cheap mattresses, counting bedbugs. The mattresses are striped. The days are long, grass is exhausted. In the bus station and in the bandstand in the park dogs lie in the shade, panting in the heat. The legs of the sleeping ones twitch. Pigeons roost in a bedroom where a window has been left open. They stain the brocade. The secret policemen have been laid off; walking home, one spits on his badge and polishes it with the hem of his shirt. No rush hour, no queues at the check-outs, no scrum at the turnstiles, no children bunking off school, no early-morning joggers, no insomniacs cursing the moon, no witnesses — not a bad time to slip in a quick killing. No distractions — also a good time, surely, to get some writing done.

*

Confusion. Not panic, though the boy who knocked on my door at around 5 a.m. was clearly in a hurry. He took from his pocket a crushed yellow beret – he was showing me that he is Lee's son. Late teens, same colour eyes. Scar on his cheek. He speaks very little English. He was frightened but I sensed this was nothing new. He handed me a battered rucksack into which I packed a few clothes. The plastic clip was broken, wouldn't close. I kept trying, uselessly – if only I could get that clip to fasten then everything would click into place. I gave up. Then I knocked on Mike's door but the boy shook his head and pulled me to another door that opened onto the stairwell. A lot of stairs, so many floors, and I got into a rhythm – after days of inactivity I was enjoying this – *faster, faster!* We exited into the underground car park, where a man was waiting on a motorbike with a side-car like Steve McQueen's in *The Great Escape*. We set off to the train station.

Laptops, headphones: there's a studious quiet in the train as in a room in which students are taking an exam, heads down, whether a draughty Portakabin or a wood-panelled hall with portraits of ancient dull men hung high on the walls. No one will fail.

Still rain, frantic on the windows. We speed through the suburbs, the names of outlying stations an illegible blur on the platforms, and then past warehouses, service stations, silos . . . A scrapyard for dead cars, vans, trucks and buses stacked in teetering piles. Generations of them: ziggurats. Is *this* the recycling centre? Large black birds circling overhead – vultures? It goes on for miles and rather than ending it segues into undulating hills of landfill refuse: mattresses, bedsteads, sofas, dressing gowns, obsolete hardware, bottles, washing machines, packaging, breakfast cereals, cat litter, incontinence pads, books, paintings, political manifestos, end-of-term reports, love letters, invoices, early drafts and final demands, everything that everyone throws out settling into a mulch of semi-decomposition and no, I cannot imagine future archaeologists sifting through this evidence and reconstructing my daily life and nor do I want that. A graveyard not for people, who are mostly organic waste, but for *stuff*. Backdrop to a fashion shoot for *Vogue*. A stage set for an opera. Chorus of cleaning women, keening. Old-school religion: plagues and curses and abominations. An oracle resides here, with demands for sacrifice: I could slit a goat's throat and ask a question and it would give me a riddling answer so smudged it can always say, whatever actually happens next, *I told you so*.

Smoke rises from the mounds, despite the rain. As far as the eye can see, and then further. On the skyline a JCB scoops, turns, deposits. Seagulls. Children foraging. Little stick figures.

Nothing new under the sun. It's bleak out there but inside the train I am comfortable and warm. Womb temperature? I could stream a movie or order *boeuf bourguignon* or file an official complaint which they will reply to within ten working days but there's a window and I am bound to spend at least part of this journey looking out of it while knowing that what I see through shatter-proof toughened glass is pre-programmed by what I have seen already or read already or have weakly imagined to be the case. And soon enough the light will play its party trick, outside fading to black and the glass framing nothing more than the reflection of a rather tired and tiresome man who happens to be me. Self as screensaver.

We were two-a-penny, Mike and I. Even if, at the reading we gave, we had swapped over, Mike reading from my work and me from his, no one apart from Lee would have noticed. Two white guys, both getting on a bit, spot the difference. Mike's prose is not good for reading aloud and mine was better, sometimes, but I'm not going to make a meal of it.

How do you know when you've finished a book, I once asked Mike, and he said something about tying up the loose ends. Mike as a Boy Scout, practising his knots. And then he asked me what colour a canary is and I didn't want to tell him that not all canaries are yellow because ornithology is not the point. When you are ready to let it go, perhaps? De-couple. Shunting yards at Clapham Junction. I'm not sure I know what feeling *ready* would feel like. I'm not sure I want to know. The look in the eyes of the skiers at the top of the slope in the Winter Olympics is chilling.

There is always something not quite there, something I know I've forgotten even if I can't remember what that thing is. Have you looked in the bathroom? people say. Or: It can't be far away. Or: It will turn up.

When people die they always leave things unfinished. The washing-up. The unpaid bills.

A black-and-white postcard of two men in peaked caps on a golf course in Scotland in the 1930s: Mike and me. For sale on eBay. Warm weak tea and sandwiches. Someone switches on the darkness.

[*Illegible*]

The rain has stopped and we are on a different train: slower, older, colder. Grimy windows, slashed seats. Fewer passengers. Crisp packets and unfiltered cigarette butts on the floor. I know this train: it's out of my childhood. But I have been let out of school: no more statistics, homework, bells, splinters, chilblains, corridors.

Seated opposite, legs sprawled. Lee's son is playing a game on his phone, rapid thumbs.

Large black animals with horns in flooded fields: cattle? Water buffalo? Gateposts. Some are leaning – *italic* gateposts. Low clouds, reluctant to move, pregnant with rain, saying we know you want to take a vintage photograph, atmospheric, elegiac, and early exposure times were long, we are trying to help. No hurry.

Farmhouses, villages, muddy roads. The windows in the houses are unglazed, vacant. Farm machinery in the fields, untended. Harrows, planters. Tanks? *Ordnance*, deployed as a solution. When a tank is hit the men inside it are burned alive. I look up, expecting to see a giant, ungainly, careless child who has dropped his toys.

The sky clears. Weak sunshine. Glitter of standing water in the fields. The train runs alongside the shore of a lake and a pack of wild dogs looks up as we pass and Lee's son puts away his phone and nods at me. And then he smiles and this is a completely new person, without fear, welcoming.

My room is monastic: thin mattress on a metal bedstead, a chair, a narrow table with two rickety drawers. Career change: I am now a monk.

On the chair someone has left a paperback novel with

yellowing pages and a receipt for a tin of paint tucked inside it. I immediately feel a sense of affinity with the previous reader and, possibly, the author.

I can see the lake, a short distance down an unpaved road, through a window that won't close because its frame is swollen and rotten. The single-floor house is raised above the ground on breezeblocks. The only heating comes from a tiled stove in the kitchen. It feels empty because more people used to live here. A row of muddy boots.

Fishing tackle. Mould. Slimy trails on the floor, still sticky – I've touched them. In one of the drawers in the table in my room, beneath a scatter of spindly white bones – fish bones? bird bones? – there is a folder of Lee's notebook sketches: Mike and me, and I recognised one or two others. They are quite famous, as writers go, or went.

Do I really look like that? I have always understood the superstition that when someone takes your likeness – a drawing, a photograph – they are stealing your soul, even though I have always insisted that I don't have a soul to be stolen. Or to sell.

Take it. Maybe you can use it better.

When we arrived a woman who I assume is Lee's mother, though she may be his grandmother or just a friend of the family, served us soup with hard bread. I wolfed it down. I couldn't recall when I had last eaten, or even when I had last spoken. When I tried to express my thanks the sound of my own voice took me by surprise.

Lying awake in the dark. Wind through the trees — music, the origin of. Just one tree will do it. The house creaks and the countryside is noisy. In the paintings of rural scenes in the national gallery the sound was turned off. Painting takes me for deaf, music takes me for blind. Most films take me for an idiot, and sometimes I'm happy with that. Many novels take me for a loner in a garret wanting communion, or a party animal who wants a quiet room, or *both*.

Among the stories are those of people who, when they wake from a coma or after a bash on the head, are able to speak an ancient language. Only a few dusty old scholars have any idea what they are saying. When they translate, it turns out to be shipping instructions.

After the trees have told me that the wind has moved on — roaming, no special place in mind — there are still rustles, scufflings, croaks. A dog barks in the road, then another, and others answer from across the lake, the sound amplified by the water.

It's when everything goes dead quiet, that's when I should start to worry.

I have been missing the sound of wind through leaves, wind in the trees and bushes. And mud, the stuff we come out of. Not the cold. It seems a lifetime since I was complaining that my room was too hot.

Despite that, I continue to think that Mike's editor should get out their their blue pencil and *wield* it. I haven't signed off yet, I am still in the game.

Genre painting: a man in the subway – or sitting on a bench in the park, if it's summer – reading a book. My tribe. Someone's ancestor.

A sweet taste in my mouth this morning translated into a deep feeling of gratitude for not having had to grow up in the middle of nowhere and for my parents not having been breeders of pedigree dogs. Industrial amounts of faeces and industrial reproduction of a species in the selective interest of flat skulls, wide eyes, obedience, profit. Lives foreshortened because of constricted breathing and back pain but people will always come back for more. The barking, the smell, the wire cages, never a day off and never becoming emotionally attached to the puppies because on Tuesday a thrilled-to-bits family will arrive from the city in their SUV and take away the cutest, and on Wednesday the next SUV and the next cutest, and so on down to the one-eyed runt. Bin-end, bargain price. But not me, they won't take *me* away.

The Scottish woman turns out to be a direct descendant of Mary Queen of Scots.

The Scottish woman was bullied at school.

The Scottish woman has had three miscarriages.

The Scottish woman is Mike's half-sister. Same father, different mother. Small world.

I make her up and pull her apart and let her go. No need: she has already moved on, she has her own life to lead.

Again, that porous patch of time, both late and early. No clocks, and my phone battery is dead. Where does Lee's son charge his own phone?

Where is Lee? I asked and they smiled at me as if I was speaking baby-talk.

And where is Lee's wife? That woman in the photograph who looked too young to be the mother of a teenage boy.

I'm nearly at the end of my notebook. Maybe Lee has left a spare sketchbook lying around. But do I really want to go on making scratches on blank white pages? Don't scratch, my mother used to say, it'll only make it worse.

I inhaled, and the sound in my head was that of an express train entering a tunnel. No one now remembers the 1860s, or even the 1910s.

I asked Lee about charging my phone. He said that he will sort it, and then he shook his head and laughed, as if he had just realised what he had taken on, and all the other things I might need.

Not his job. And I won't need much. I will go for long walks. I will help with fetching and carrying whatever they trust me not to drop. I will write letters. I will start a collection of interesting pebbles from the shore of the lake. Discover that I have a sweet tooth after all. Revert to childhood. Or I might do nothing at all, which right now I am finding very hard but it will doubtless get easier as I settle in. Early days.

No helicopters here. But still, very high and very far, some planes, their contrails scarring the sky.

Closer down, a fat, squat spider was crawling across the window sill and I was about to push it out when I recognised it – this was Mike, shapeshifting. Ugly as sin but maybe he didn't have any choice and I didn't resent him for being so unlovely, and for making me feel responsible for his safety. I moved him – tickling my palms! – into the drawer in the desk and settled him among the fine bones.

I walked out past clothes dried hard on a clothes-line. No surprises here: pot-holes, puddles, weeds, rust, litter tangled in the bushes, cans and plastic bags. The edges, where everything gets blown. A packet of crisps with salt in a tiny twirled packet of blue waxy paper – that blue was thrilling. A flickering neon light, the ₂₂₂₂₂ of faulty connection. And if this place is familiar to me then I am familiar to it. It knows me. Not inside out, not all my little grudges and fond hopes and pale regrets, thank god, but it knows my *type*. It skim-reads me. That's usually enough.

On the way back one of the village dogs approached me, sniffed, then trotted on, going its own sweet doggy way.

I'm thinking of the boy who came into my hotel room and bounced on the bed and played with the curtains. I hope he's OK. I'm thinking of the Scottish woman's sister making pancakes in Colorado. I'm thinking of Harry, and wondering what will happen to his collection of first editions after he dies. If his children think they are valuable they will be disappointed. And I'm thinking of Mike back home in Marlow pointing to his framed dog's foot on the wall and his dinner guests pretending to be interested – or perhaps they are interested, or one of them is – and Debra pouring herself another large glass of wine and then Mike takes the foot out of the frame and dangles it in front of his live dog, the one that farted and dribbled on me in the back seat of the car on the way to the airport, and the dog of course sniffs it but is too honest to feign any further interest. Nothing here to eat. Nothing to fuck.

I remember Lee struggling to open a bottle of mineral water. You have to split the little plastic seal, somehow. The seal is there to prevent people with grudges against society in general from poisoning me in particular and may also be a metaphor for something or other. This was at the stand outside the hotel where we were waiting for our car, the place where I saw Mike having a tug-of-war with his woman, the kind of *liminal* space the cool guys used to write essays about. It was starting to rain. But he wouldn't let anyone help him.

I remember Lucy, I remember the *smell* of that dog as well as the torn ear and the blind eye, but I don't remember ever hearing that dog bark. Too enfeebled, too far gone? The sound of Lucy's bark would be like a human – me, for example – mimicking a dog's bark. That dog must be dead by now, shovelled into a ditch.

I have made a list of the brand names of all the chocolate bars from my childhood. It would be a longer list if there was someone else here of roughly my own age and background to help me, but all lists are incomplete. And another list of the names of all the dogs I had as a child. Mike was right to be dubious about the story of the first one being poisoned by gypsies. Probably it was just run over by a car and my parents didn't want to tell me that death can be so random so they made up a story involving malicious intent. I wonder at how much I have believed to be the case simply because I was told this by people I trusted.

Lee's son looks at me as if he's about to say something and then doesn't. His resemblance to his father is uncanny. I think he thinks I need a girlfriend but he doesn't know where to find one, and nor do I.

His English isn't up to fluent translation but it doesn't matter. Here, there is less to say. No, *more*, if I'm being honest, which is what diaries are supposed to be for, but saying it seems beside the point.

I have stopped dreaming. Or remembering my dreams; but I think it's not me, it's the dreams themselves that have stopped. The whole network is down. It was always pretty ropy: I often suspected that the dreams I was dreaming were not really mine, they were someone else's. A few wires had got crossed.

If . . . I would pay more attention. Ask better questions. Be more kind. Be less self-deceived. All of that. I would sing more, and dance.

Mr Jackson looks sceptical.

I looked through a window in the village school and there he was, sitting at a table in front of rows of desks and empty chairs. A bit older, a bit heavier, a bit grumpier. Very slowly he was taking exercise books from a pile on his left, opening them and making ticks or crosses, and placing them on another, smaller pile on his right. He was marking homework. He is left-handed.

The dogs that flipped around a corner, the dogs that Lee said didn't exist – I used to wonder what they found there. A posse of other dogs? A heap of bones? The edge of a cliff, the limits of human knowledge? Cookham? The artist Stanley Spencer, who rarely ventured beyond his native village of Cookham in Berkshire, felt at home in China in 1954 'because I feel that Cookham is somewhere near, only just around the corner'. A cobbler's, a hardware shop, a woman taking off her gloves in the bakery to count her change, a grey (but everything is grey) Austin A35 parked in front of a tea shop, a muddy path along the river bank. A lamp post, a black dog, a cocked leg. A bag of stale bread for feeding the ducks. A jamjar to catch tadpoles. No litter bins because on a damp afternoon in the early 1950s wartime rationing of foods and petrol is still in force and thrift was a national habit, people didn't throw things away. Litter bins came later, in a time of surfeit; and then are removed, because terrorists might plant bombs in them.

I have a problem with tenses, I need an editor. Wayward tenses: essay? I also need a new agent. And Lee's mother has decided I need a haircut. Tufts of my hair drift down to the damp floorboards, whiter than I'd thought. I would like to be the boy who sweeps them up, overhears the gossip, refills the bottles of gel, spray-cleans the mirror, job done, *'Next!'*

Lying on my back on my mattress, I count four spiders scuttling among the rafters above me. One of them is Mike but from here I can't tell which.

Outside, someone is sweeping the yard with a stiff broom.

The president too is in exile, and I imagine his bed is more comfortable than mine but I don't envy him. I imagine that he lives in a hot, hot country in a heavily guarded compound in a pale, rich suburb, and I imagine that his cook is French and his security guards are Russian and his bank accounts are Swiss because these are the tropes and not without reason and I imagine that in the early evenings when the sun slopes down, clocks off for the day, he goes for a splash in his private swimming pool. I can see his belly overlapping his swimming trunks, a generic late-middle-age belly, but I can't see his face because even on TV we never actually *saw* the president. And there were dogs too that I didn't see, quite apart from the ones I did see but officially didn't. Secret dogs. Dogs behind a pay-wall. Whatever is forbidden becomes desirable, and therefore a form of currency, and at the time of the great cull those who kept dogs as pets and who had the means to do this hid their dogs away; others kidnapped stray pups from the streets as an investment . . . Some of those dogs were conditioned – brutalised, starved – to take part in dog-fights in off-the-record locations and make money for their owners. Fistfuls of grubby banknotes changed hands. Protection rackets, extortion, disappearances, *omertà*. The dogs concealed by the rich, meanwhile, were pampered: expensive grooming and prime cuts of meat in the locked rooms of the villas and penthouse apartments where they were kept. Live small animals were chucked into those rooms: the dogs needed exercise. Most had their vocal cords cut to stop them barking and attracting unwelcome attention. The dogs were status symbols among the elite. White truffles and imported cars, these counted, but only a dog proved that you were above the law.

A currency, as I say, and the pampered dogs and the brutalised dogs were two sides of the same coinage. They kept to their own sides in public but in private they kissed. They did more than kiss: they got into bed. The president, I now understand, and the chief of police and the head of intelligence and the minister of culture, were *dogs* – dogs from the pampered class who had turned upon their complacent human masters all their rage at confinement and tedium and mindless luxury, dogs with passable social graces, having been raised in top-drawer households, but who depended on the brutalised dogs to maintain power. Lee never stood a chance.

I had a parting in my hair. Clean your shoes, I was told. And take off your hat indoors, and open doors for ladies, and never shoot a man in the back.

I shout at Lee's mother. She has shorn me. I look like crew-cut conscript cannon-fodder for a colonial war, I look like a collaborator who's had their hair scissored off in public for sleeping with the enemy, I look like an urchin in a workhouse, a plucked chicken in the market, a shaved patient on the operating table, I look like a prisoner on death row and I may deserve to be there but that doesn't make it any less terrible. I shout at Lee's mother and she doesn't flinch and Lee's son stares at me, afraid, the anger inside me a surprise to us both.

'Mike was on song tonight.' 'But he left early. Did someone say something? He can be touchy.' 'Who was that woman he came with? She was lovely.' The post-mortem: a last drink at the kitchen table after the guests have all gone home. The window open, candles guttering. The clearing-up can be left till tomorrow. The child

listening at the door, his presence sensed by his mother
— a glass of cold milk from the fridge, then back to bed
with a kiss.

Early morning at the lakeside. Paw-prints in the sand.
The hills are hidden by mist but I know you are there,
even though I can't see you. Birdsong — invisible birds. I
strip off and enter the water, which is soft, like wool, and
not as cold as I'd feared.

The towel is threadbare and scratchy. Mike would be
complaining but I prefer it to the towels we had in the
hotel, which were made out of marshmallow.

My razor must have fallen out of the rucksack with
the broken clip as I was rushing down the stairs in the
hotel. Or it's still on the basin in the bathroom: I can see
it from four different angles, in the mirrors.

Afterword

> At this point Kublai Khan interrupted him or imagined
> interrupting him, or Marco Polo imagined himself interrupted,
> with a question such as: 'You advance always with your head
> turned back?'
>
> — Italo Calvino, *Invisible Cities* (1974; trans. William Weaver)

Roland Barthes in China needs to go to the loo but finds the
toilet block occupied by three men 'having a shit, collectively.
They don't seem in much of a hurry.'[1] On the same day he is
invited to relax in the Emperor's bath – 'but it turns out that
it's being repaired'. . . Much of travel is frustration, and much
of the appeal of travel writing is that it delivers the comedy of
this. Delays, cancellations, mechanical breakdowns, bad food,
bad weather, bad timing: Albert Camus flies across the Andes
in 1949 at night and 'I can't see a thing – which just about sums
up this trip.'[2] Communication muddles: the replies to questions
asked by Barthes constitute 'a sort of monstrous ventriloquism'.
Travel is also tiredness, exhaustion, insect bites, sea-sickness,
headaches, insomnia, diarrhoea and fever. Albert Einstein on
a boat in the Red Sea in 1923: 'Enteritis with ghastly haemor-
rhoids. Japanese professor comes to the rescue.'[3] And disorien-
tation, derailment and depression. Camus again ('I'm writing
this in the plane to São Paulo'): 'What finally seemed clear to
me yesterday is that I wish to die.'

The comedy is often black. The wish to die crops up often.
In 1941 Martha Gellhorn endured a nightmare trip with Ernest

Hemingway to China: 'It was very cold. The door opened on to the street and the smell thereof. The mosquitoes were competing with the flies and losing . . . I lay on my boards, a foot off the floor, and said in the darkness: "I wish to die."'[4] The following morning she is stuck up a ladder on the village latrine, a bamboo tower erected over a large pot that collected human manure, during a Japanese air raid. Hemingway takes shelter until the planes have passed, and then remarks: 'O poor M, what an inglorious death it would have been.'

Most of the travel diaries I've been reading are those of white, male, European writers venturing into countries beyond their ken; most of them date from that period in the recent past – but it already feels almost medieval – when Western writers were seen as *influencers* and deployed overseas as soft power.[5] The diaries were written up in notebooks on the road or late at night in hotel rooms, and not for publication – that came later, with introductions and footnotes by editors who often struggled with the authors' handwriting. And more than the handwriting: in their introduction to the first volume of Einstein's travel diaries the editors acknowledge that Einstein 'advocated an "enlightened" form of colonialism, and did not always accept the basic humanity of the local populaces'.

Roland Barthes travelled to China in 1974 with four companions, three of them associated with the *Tel Quel* literary magazine, which had broken with the French Communist Party and declared for Maoism. They followed a strict itinerary: factories and dockyards, operas and ballets, museums and tourist sites. Barthes was diligent, bored and sexually frustrated. He didn't have to travel halfway around the world to be those things but having done so, he wrote it all down, and *Travels in China*, his diary notes published thirty years after his death, is a self-portrait of a writer adrift, a lost boy.

Quite how lost was discerned by Simon Leys, who noted that Barthes' visit to China 'coincided with a colossal, bloody purge launched nation-wide by the Maoist regime'.[6] Barthes' diary contains page after page of statistics transcribed from propaganda lectures and no mention at all of any purge.

'What people believe is essentially what they wish to believe,' Leys observes wearily in an essay on Western intellectuals who got Maoism wrong (Barthes was far from the only one), and they generally see what they want to see, or are told to see, rather than what is staring them in the face. Leys points to the usual human muddle of idealism and cynicism, generosity and self-interest, cleverness and stupidity, but for travellers in strange lands there is also this: because they *don't know where they are going*, to get their bearings they are constantly looking over their shoulders.

Patrick Wright's *Passport to Peking* documents three delegations from the UK to China in 1954.[7] Two comprised Labour politicians and trades-union officials; the members of the third, a 'cultural' delegation, included the philosopher A. J. Ayer, the architect Hugh Casson, the writer Rex Warner and the artist Stanley Spencer, who kept asking waiters to bring him toast and eggs. Of the thirty-four delegates in the three groups, three were female. Wright notes how often these Englishmen (plus a woman or two) abroad, trying to describe what they were seeing, referred backwards: a Chinese port city like 'a South Coast English seaside resort whose better days lay at the beginning of the century'; arriving in Shanghai 'like pulling into Manchester from Sheffield'; landscapes 'reminiscent of the Midlands'; Moscow in 1954 looking 'like Manchester a century ago'. His book, Wright states, is 'far more about post-war Britain and its inherited perspectives than it is about the reality of China, either now or then'.

Along with a change of socks and underwear, inherited perspectives – inclusive of prejudices and blind spots – are in the backpacks of all travellers; those greeting them have their own expectations and suspicions. The awkwardness of advancing while facing backwards is inescapable. ('The right gaze,' Barthes suggests, with insistent italics, 'is *a sideways gaze*.') How do I reckon the new without comparing it to what I already know? Both travel and fiction – and fictional travels, from Jonathan Swift to Calvino – can suggest I don't even know *that*.

Not knowing is a good place to start from, and sometimes to go back to. Travel has ways of pitching us there.

NOTES

1. Roland Barthes, *Travels in China* (trans. Andrew Brown; Polity Press, 2012).

2. *The Travel Diaries of Albert Einstein: The Far East, Palestine & Spain 1922–1923* (ed. Ze'ev Rosenkranz; Princeton University Press, 2018).

3. Albert Camus, *Travels in the Americas* (ed. Alice Kaplan, trans. Ryan Bloom; University of Chicago Press, 2023).

4. Martha Gellhorn, *Travels with Myself and Another* (Eland, 1978).

5. A mission statement in the 1940/41 annual report of the British Council spoke of creating overseas 'a friendly knowledge and

understanding [. . .] which will lead to a sympathetic appreciation of British foreign policy, whatever for the moment that policy may be'. In the 1950s and 60s the London-based literary and cultural journal *Encounter*, whose contributors included leading British writers and academics, was covertly funded by the CIA. The more cultural importance is claimed for literature, not least by writers themselves, the more it is played by power-mongers.

6. Simon Leys, 'Roland Barthes in China', in *The Hall of Uselessness: Collected Essays* (NYRB, 2013). Also in there is the other essay by Leys cited above, 'The Curse of the Man Who Could See the Little Fish at the Bottom of the Ocean'.

7. Patrick Wright, *Passport to Peking: A Very British Mission to Mao's China* (OUP, 2010).

Ⓑ *editions*

Founded in 2007, CB editions publishes
chiefly short fiction and poetry, including
work in translation. Books can be ordered
from www.cbeditions.com.